BABY, IT'S MURDER
A MIKE HAMMER NOVEL

MORE MIKE HAMMER
FROM TITAN BOOKS

Lady, Go Die!
Complex 90
King of the Weeds
Kill Me, Darling
Murder Never Knocks
The Will to Kill
Killing Town
The Goliath Bone
Murder, My Love
The Big Bang
Kiss Her Goodbye
Masquerade for Murder
Dig Two Graves

BABY, IT'S MURDER

A MIKE HAMMER NOVEL

MICKEY SPILLANE
and
MAX ALLAN COLLINS

TITANBOOKS

Baby, It's Murder: A Mike Hammer Novel
Print edition ISBN: 9781803364599
E-book edition ISBN: 9781803364605

Published by Titan Books
A division of Titan Publishing Group Ltd
144 Southwark Street, London SE1 0UP
www.titanbooks.com

First edition: March 2025
10 9 8 7 6 5 4 3 2 1

This is a work of fiction. All of the characters, organizations, and events portrayed in this novel are either products of the author's imagination or are used fictitiously. Any resemblance to actual persons, living or dead (except for satirical purposes), is entirely coincidental.

© 2025 Mickey Spillane Publishing, LLC

Mickey Spillane and Max Allan Collins assert the moral right to be identified as the authors of this work.

No part of this publication may be reproduced, stored in a retrieval system, or transmitted, in any form or by any means without the prior written permission of the publisher, nor be otherwise circulated in any form of binding or cover other than that in which it is published and without a similar condition being imposed on the subsequent purchaser.

A CIP catalogue record for this title is available from the British Library.

Printed and bound by CPI Group (UK) Ltd, Croydon, CR0 4YY

For

MICKEY and **JANE** —

thanks for believing in me.

"Nobody reads a mystery
to get to the middle."
Mickey Spillane

"I think there are certain crimes
which the law cannot touch,
and which therefore
justify private revenge."
Sir Arthur Conan Doyle

CO-AUTHOR'S INTRODUCTION

Shortly before his death in 2006, Mickey Spillane gave me an assignment – develop decades' worth of various uncompleted manuscripts and synopses of his into completed form for publication.

Several reasons are behind the surprising number of manuscripts the bestselling mystery writer of his day left unfinished. One is his struggle with balancing his new-found (circa 1953) religious beliefs with the sex-and-violence reputation his fiction engendered. The major reason, perhaps – revealed in my biography *Spillane: King of Pulp Fiction* (co-written with James L. Traylor) – is Mickey's contract with director/producer Victor Saville granting the filmmaker screen rights to any yet unwritten Hammer (and other) crime novels.

Mike Hammer's creator disliked the Spillane-derived films Saville made, although Mickey came to appreciate the enduring importance of director Robert Aldrich's *Kiss Me Deadly* (1955), that fascinating film in which a critique of Mike Hammer somehow perfectly captures the feel of the initial six Hammer novels.

At the time, however, Mickey simply waited out the duration of the Saville contract before returning to his famous detective with the novel *The Girl Hunters* (1962), which led to Spillane portraying Hammer himself in the 1963 film version, which he co-produced.

Baby, It's Murder is the fifteenth Mike Hammer novel I've developed from unfinished, previously unpublished Spillane material found in the files of his three offices at his South Carolina home after an extensive search by his wife Jane, my wife Barb and myself. These ranged from substantial manuscripts – running to a hundred or more type-written pages, sometimes with plot notes and occasionally roughed-out endings – to one-page synopses for proposed Stacy Keach TV movies, and many stops between. This concluding Hammer novel was developed from several opening chapters and some plot notes.

Continuity is always an issue in Spillane's Hammer, because the writer (never "author") had a tendency to pay only lip service to it. On the other hand – unusual for a detective series – the impact of events from previous novels is often felt in subsequent ones. Deep into Spillane's Hammer series, for example, the detective still feels guilt and loss over the femme fatale he dispatches at the end of *I, the Jury* (1947). So, in that sense, continuity was important to Spillane.

The bulk of the action in *Baby, It's Murder* takes place in the early 1970s; but the framing sequences occur in the early 2000s, chronologically after what had previously been the final Hammer novel, *The Goliath Bone*: the first posthumous Hammer novel (and the first with a shared Spillane/Collins byline).

Completing the unfinished Hammer books has been both a challenge and a delight. Along the way I have also completed the long-anticipated second Morgan the Raider novel (*The Consummata*, a sequel to *The Delta Factor*); Mickey's nearly finished last crime novel, *Dead Street*; and edited his final completed work, *The Last Stand*, all for Hard Case Crime. Additionally, two novels were developed from unproduced Spillane screenplays (*The Menace* and *The Saga of Caleb York*, the latter leading to a six-novel western series). And enough Hammer short stories were completed from shorter fragments to fill *A Long Time Dead: A Mike Hammer Casebook*.

That Mickey himself, shortly before his passing, asked me to undertake this mission is the biggest compliment I have ever received. That so many readers have accepted these collaborations as genuine Spillane novels is the best review I could ever hope for.

I am grateful to Nick Landau, Vivian Cheung, and Andrew Sumner, as well as Laura Price and the rest of the Titan Books staff, for their belief and support in the Mickey Spillane's Mike Hammer Legacy Project. Mysterious Press editor/publisher Otto Penzler played a key role as well. All of you stayed the distance, understanding the importance to mystery fiction of sharing with readers these additional, final works from one of the genre's key creators.

Max Allan Collins
July 2024

PROLOGUE

An NYPD chaplain officiated at the graveside ceremony, as per Velda's wishes. She had, after all, been a policewoman once, before she became the other licensed investigator in the Hammer agency. She could also have asked for, and received, a military send-off, because her remarkable heroic life had included service with the Central Intelligence Agency.

A heroine's send-off was what she rated, after living a lifetime with me. We'd only married a few years ago, but we'd been together for decades prior, sharing a business, living in the same apartment building, then the same apartment, and finally retiring to beachfront Florida, an old married couple. But she'd made it clear, when the finality of the doctor's diagnosis made the inevitable sooner than later, that she would lay to rest in Manhattan, where she had only occasionally rested in a lifetime of activity.

A heroine's life.

About an equivalent of a third of the living population of Manhattan already rested here. It was a popular place, Green-Wood Cemetery. And why not? Trees everywhere, half-a-million or so acres of rolling hills and dales, an occasional pond, a chapel. I'd been here *visiting dead friends — Jack Williams was here — back when you could hardly move left or right without running into gravediggers, and nothing spoils a cemetery visit like running into one of those.*

But now the diggers seemed almost rare — not much space left for burials. Dying is costly these days. They'd taken to stacking family members like pancakes in some plots, presumably minus syrup. Of course, Velda had planned ahead. She'd reserved a space for me, as well. My name was next to hers on the gravestone, with a place waiting for the eventual death date to be carved in.

Don't be impatient, doll, *I thought.* I'll be there soon enough.

For such a beautiful burying place, the day had insisted on a melancholy mien, as if the sky was sorry to see her go, too. The gray was gentle, though, not threatening rain, just respecting and protecting the sorrow of the day with a balmy breeze, an umbrella courtesy of God, a final kiss courtesy of Velda.

Looking like a movie star who'd aged well, Pat Chambers, the longtime captain of Homicide who'd finally made inspector before they retired him out, had made the trip from Florida, too. He and the ex-policewoman wife he'd finally found — his love for Velda paying off only in friendship — were a couple with whom we'd often socialized; they were in Key West and we weren't far from there. We'd play cards and reminisce, and our wives would try (rarely successfully) to curtail how much Miller beer we imbibed.

Pat's wife hadn't made the trip. She knew something very personal bound Pat, Velda and me, and she paid her respects by keeping her distance.

The funeral had been held at the Green-Wood chapel, and the place had been packed. That had surprised me, though it shouldn't have. I'd figured a couple of dinosaurs like Mike and Velda Hammer, however well-preserved the former Miss Sterling had been, would be very old news in the town with so much vice they named it twice.

But people with whom our lives had intersected, people she had touched and their children and their children's children, surprised us with their sorrow and support, and many accompanied us to the graveside, an army of appreciation.

Pat *really* had *loved* Vel, and his eyes were brimming with tears that never quite made their escape. I was less manly about it. I held up through the service just fine, and even laughed at some of the anecdotes that got told by friends invited up to share their memories. Velda and I knew professional comedians and showbiz columnists who could work a crowd, particularly a sentimental one like this. And they scored big. People needed to laugh.

Then when that fucking dark hole yawned at me, and slowly swallowed the simple bronze casket she'd insisted upon, and after I tossed in the requisite handful of dirt, the rains came — not the sky's, but mine. It took blowing my nose to return to my reputation as the hard-ass who Mike Hammer was supposed to be.

We were walking away, Pat and me, when he spotted her. I'd noticed Mikki at the chapel. We'd nodded at each other. We were close but not that close.

"My God," Pat breathed, "that gave me a start."

"Remarkable, isn't it?"

He might have seen a ghost. "I thought it was her for a moment. I thought it was Velda."

"No. Her sister. Mikki. Named for her grandfather, Michael Sterling. Mike. Like me. He was a longshoreman, not a sissy P.I."

"What a lovely woman."

And she was, all in form-fitting black, but no veil of affectation – the same sleek black style-defying page boy, the dark, slightly Asian eyes, the full lips, the figure that could stop traffic, even a funeral procession.

I said, "I'll introduce you."

He raised a traffic-cop palm. "No need – I remember meeting her when she was young. Would *like* to say hello." He shook his head. "I'd damn near forgotten all of that. That business on Long Island."

"Long time ago, Pat."

"Everything was. A long time ago."

CHAPTER ONE

They were backed up against a fence at the dead-end of a Greenwich Village brick alley, three over-age hippies, one Black and the other two White, in thrift-store garb that would have been perfect if this were Halloween, their breaths visible clouds of fear in the gray chill of this late March afternoon.

With a back-up team coming in on the other side of the fence, the stupid ofay bastard in a fringed buckskin jacket and a Gabby Hayes beard carried the paper bag in one fist like it was a dog-shit surprise he was lugging to a porch, while in his other hand he clutched a big revolver. He turned and so did the buckskin fringe, like a dog's hackles rising, and he triggered off two shots that went right between me and Captain Pat Chambers of the NYPD Homicide Bureau, coming up on the trio at a run. The reporter from the *News*, who'd been with us from the start, yiped like he'd been hit – though he hadn't been. But I bet he peed a little.

I kept coming and squeezed off the .45 automatic's trigger, a gentle action that created a thunderous echo in the alley accompanying the slug, catching the grocery-bag idiot right in the chest, tearing on through to hit the remaining white boy in the head and splashing the fence with red and green and gray matter that dripped like wet paint. The soul brother was reaching down for the first faux-hippie's fallen rod when I had to drop him, too. I tried for a leg shot but he had bent down too damn low and he caught it from right to left through the lungs.

Pat and I came to a stop.

"Shit," I said.

Two bullets and five seconds were all it took for them to die.

"Please don't tell me you're sorry," Pat said, trotting over to the corpses littering the alley and/or bumping up against a fence they'd never get over. Boys in blue were peeking over that fence like kids at a ballpark.

"I was hoping one would survive," I said. My attitude was clinical. "Might get us a rung up the connection ladder."

Reporters who carry cameras like something precious they won are all lunatics and the automated Nikon that Ray Giles carried, no matter how scared shitless he was, lit up the scene a dozen times, getting it all down in glorious black and white – if his city editor would go for so much gore on the hoof.

The three-man back-up team in blue clambered up and over the fence. The first man to drop skidded in the blood smear and damn near fell on his ass on the alley's brick.

I chuckled and Captain Chambers – my oldest living friend on the planet, helming a joint Narcotics and Homicide Squad task force – pushed his out-of-date fedora back on his blond head and said, "Some sick damn sense of humor you got, Mike."

I pushed my porkpie hat back in solidarity. "Aw, lighten up, Pat. These three are no great loss to humanity."

We were both in trench coats, looking like twins only he was a much better-looking slob. Sort of Alan Ladd if the actor had been taller.

He was giving me that grave look I knew so well. "You're not official here, my friend. You may have got yourself in a world of hurt this time. There's a new D.A. in town, you know."

"There's always a new D.A. in town. I'm here as a duly licensed bodyguard for a *News* reporter, and I'm an officer of the court to boot. And I have a witness named Chambers who can verify one of those dead pricks shot first."

He could find no argument with any of that.

Giles was done strobing the scene with his Nikon; he was shaking so bad, it was a miracle he'd held the camera steady. He was prematurely bald, a baby bird with a mustache and thinning hair; his suit had a whipped look like he just made it alive out of a twister. "Did you have to kill 'em all, Mike?"

I shrugged. "So I missed. Anyway, did I have a choice?"

Giles must have still had some of the sound of those slugs whistling past his head, ears ringing from the reverberation blast of my big automatic. "Not *this* time, Mike."

The press and the cops had some ideas about the figurative notches on my .45. Robin Hood had a bow and arrow; Mike Hammer packed a Colt 1911.

The uniform boys were holding back the gathering crowd, white eyes in faces of various color lighting up the descending night. From the surf-like collective murmur came an occasional, "That's Mike Hammer!" "No, can't be. Isn't he dead?" "No, I tell you it's Mike Hammer!" At least one of them was right.

We walked up to the mess at alley's end and, in the glare of a couple of flashlights two of the uniformed guys were wielding now that dark was settling in, I watched while Pat knelt over the paper bag and snugged his hands into latex gloves, then opened up on contents that were not groceries. He let Giles take a shot of the piles of glassine packets the bag held, then Ray grabbed another of Pat tasting the stuff with the tip of his tongue.

"Worth dying over?" I asked cheerfully.

Pat, on his feet again, said, "Pure heroin, I'd say. Purest stuff I've seen in a long time. Not cut with quinine at all."

"Street value?"

"Cut for the buying class, I'd say you're looking at a grocery bag worth, oh… a cool million."

Giles lowered his camera for once. His baby face cinched up like he was just learning to think. He'd hired me after I shot two others in a tenement buy I'd stumbled onto a few weeks ago, chasing down a deadbeat dad. I always did have a lucky streak.

"That's five men you killed," Giles said, half appalled, utterly impressed, "in less than a month. How does that make you feel?"

I knew anything I said would go right into the *News*, which was jake with me.

"I feel just fine."

The reporter goggled at me. "Really?"

"All of us get high one way or another," I said. "Mine is taking out scum. How do *you* feel, Ray, now that you finally made the bullet-alley scene?"

His lips were dry under the mustache and he looked pale as milk but not near as healthy. Slugs whizzing past you can do that.

"Lucky, Mike. Lucky to be alive."

Sirens were splitting the night. On their hurry here, though I didn't see the rush.

"That's great, kid," I said. "Just don't make this kind of thing your drug of choice."

This time the inquiry was fast and to the point. After all, they had a reliable witness in Ray Giles whose photos were nicely specific and his knowledge of what had gone down too intimate to turn me into the gun-happy fanatic the media liked to make of me. For a change the press got off my back and didn't harp on the other times the ultimate pay-off had happened to drug pushers who got into my line of sight. In Giles they had one of their own who had damn near tasted a few grains of hot lead.

In the hallway after the inquiry, Giles said, "You saved my life, Mike. I do appreciate that."

"No extra charge. Anyway, that asshole couldn't shoot worth a damn."

"I don't know how my editor's going to feel about it."

I put a hand on the diminutive reporter's shoulder. "He wasn't there, was he?"

"She."

I shrugged. "She wasn't there, either."

Not that in the aftermath I got any hero treatment from the *News*, much less respect, or any other sheet for that matter – just a general wait-and-see attitude with some put-down from the more liberal rags, commentators wondering whether that notorious self-appointed arbiter of rough justice had come out of his semi-retirement to start making bloody headlines again. Hell, anybody who ever had a kid hyped up on the big H or floating off on acid wouldn't bother paying any attention to the naysayers at all.

At least I had the satisfaction of knowing I'd helped Pat generate the kind of hysteria down on the streets that would follow those three dealers going down.

Of course, those three buying it was just the icing on the cake. Wednesday, nine kilos had been confiscated at Kennedy; Thursday, Union County coppers in Jersey had lopped off a major consignment being run into Teterboro Airport; and Friday, the feds hit a ship that had held sixty-seven-and-a-half pounds of pure uncut stuff in a barrel at a Brooklyn pier.

A week later, I was sitting across from the captain of Homicide in his Centre Street office, an ancient space as cluttered as Pat's mind was not. The room looked smaller than it was, thanks to the supplemental materials stacked here and there, plus we were crowded by a whiteboard that listed the various confiscations and arrests the task force had made happen since its inception.

"A key shipment," he said, between draws on his pipe, in his shirt sleeves and loosened tie, "is a day overdue for delivery. The junkies are going green, looking for connections."

I snorted a laugh as I lit up a smoke. "Well, isn't that just too fucking bad."

"Haven't you heard, Mike? Addiction is a disease."

If there was any sarcasm in that, I wasn't a good enough detective to find it.

I waved the match out, tossed it in an ashtray on the edge of some piled files. "My heart bleeds. Let them hurt right down to their squishy little balls."

He winced, as if the pipe had gone sour. "Come on, Mike – it's the suppliers who—"

I held up a stop palm. "Don't blame the suppliers, Pat, because they wouldn't be in business if they didn't have a market to feed and, as far as I'm concerned, anybody who wants to load their guts up with that shit can die in their *own* runny shit. Nobody forced them to stick that foul stuff in their veins – it was their own stupid choice. Tomorrow the street cleaners'll be scraping them off the sidewalks with the rest of the dog crap."

His sigh was as long-suffering as they come. "Listen, Mike. Your bodyguard duties for the *News* team digging into the narcotics scene have gotten entirely out of hand. Let me and the narco task force handle it. Your involvement ends here, or—"

"Else?" I blew a smoke ring. "Don't worry about it, Pat."

His smirk spoke volumes. "When Mike Hammer's your best friend, a guy tends to worry pretty much all the damn time."

"Well, you can stop. The *News* fired me."

His eyes widened. "Oh?"

I shrugged. "Or I should say thanked me for my services and gave me a cool, brief handshake. Yeah, and a check, so all's right with the world."

"Why fire you?" What came next was an admission: "If you hadn't been in that alley, Ray Giles might be dead now."

For all his bitching, Pat wouldn't have wanted to be running down an alley after armed men with anybody else but yours truly.

"That's just it," I said. "Giles has been on the crime beat long enough to've seen his share of DBs. But he isn't used to seeing guys die right in front of him. Cold stiffs is one thing – warm corpses is another."

Pat actually smiled a little. "And Giles isn't used to having bullets fly around his journalistic brow. Yeah, I get that. Winning a Pulitzer doesn't mean much when you're nailed into a box."

I shrugged, sighed. Got to my feet. "Afraid I'm back investigating insurance claims and looking for runaways for parents who should've paid more attention when their offspring were growing up. Little jobs for little people. What the hell? That's Hammer Investigations, all right. Friend to the little guy."

He stood; apparently I was being seen out. "That's rich, coming from a misanthrope like you."

"No, you underestimate my vocabulary. I like people just fine. At a distance."

He held the pipe in his palm by the bowl in that paternal way of his. "I know what your problem is."

"Yeah? Enlighten me."

"Without Velda around, you're one cranky son of a bitch."

Some things you can't argue with. "Her at my side does take the edge off," I admitted. "Spend enough time with that doll and I'm damn near human."

We were moving along the edge of the bullpen now; things were hopping, as usual.

At the elevator, Pat asked, "So how long is that lovely secretary of yours gonna be on this leave of absence?"

Now I was the one letting out a long-suffering sigh. "However long she needs. Rest of her sister's school year, maybe. Maybe all summer after that. With her mom in that nursing home, recovering, and her high-schooler sis Mikki at home... who knows?"

"Why don't you take a leave of absence from your shitty attitude and go help Vel out? You got money in the bank. You're the most successful small agency in Manhattan, thanks to all the gory press you used to get."

"And now I'm just a has-been, huh?"

He shrugged. "You made a comeback lately, like in that alley. Tell your mean-ass boss, that Hammer character, you need a break. You have a bad case of missing Velda."

No question about that — Velda was much more than just my secretary. Love of my excuse for a life, was more like it. And Pat knew whereof he spoke — he had a yen for that female himself. It caused a rift in our friendship, once upon a time, in a violent fairy tale long ago. Healed up now. Scarred over maybe, but healed up.

The elevator dinged its arrival.

"I don't think so, Pat," I said. "Who's going to keep Manhattan safe if I'm not on the job?"

I tipped my porkpie and got on the elevator, the doors closing on his smiling, shaking head.

"You are still a pisser, Mike Hammer."

"I try," I said.

CHAPTER TWO

Eight-oh-eight, the two-office suite on the eighth floor of the Hackard Building in Manhattan, had never been anything fancy, not even after the old structure had been remodeled from head to toe. A dame that old never looks any better after the surgeon's knife, but at least MICHAEL HAMMER INVESTIGATIONS didn't look any older than your random Gabor sister.

The outer office was larger than my inner one, with a couch against the right side wall as you came in, a few reception chairs, and a little table for coffee and snacks opposite. The big wooden desk opposite the entry, serving as the barrier to my inner sanctum, bore a few personal items – a framed family photo, a vase usually adorned by a few flowers but just an empty vessel currently, a blotter, pen-and-pencil cup, and a modern IBM Selectric that seemed wrong for an ancient chunk of wood that was damn near as scarred up as yours truly. This in a room whose stingy array of windows included Venetian blinds making '40s crime-movie patterns on the walls.

Still, this was a modest space even if right now it seemed cavernously empty. The coffee maker was just this cold cylinder of steel, the only fragrance touching the air an unpleasant chemical one courtesy of the Hackard janitorial staff. Morning sunlight floated with dust motes and, just a week since she left, a fine coating of the stuff reminded the man who paid the rent here that he'd never run a dust-cloth across anything in the place ever. Only she had.

She.

Velda.

That was a picture of her there on the desk – *her* desk – but its presence did not represent an out-of-control ego, though she looked typically lovely in the photo, all that raven hair in its style-defying page boy and the big, slightly Asian-looking brown eyes, those full red-lipsticked lips any movie goddess might envy. No, this was a family portrait – Velda, her matronly mother Mildred, and her sister Mikki, just an adolescent here but a young woman now. A beauty who one day might rival her older sister.

This outer office, which dwarfed my inner one, had never seemed particularly large to me. No need. A private detective's office doesn't get much walk-in trade; it doesn't need to echo a doctor's reception area, even if the customers also have afflictions that need attention. Now, however, it seemed a vast hollow shell, so empty without the woman who guarded my gate.

Seated behind her desk, I absorbed the emptiness. My eyes traveled to the little coffee-and-snacks table, and like a ghost shimmering into solidity, there she was. Not her, of course. But the memory of her, not long ago.

"You'll be fine without me," Velda said. "If this lasts longer than a few weeks, you can get a temp in."

"Temps don't pack cute little automatics in their purse," I'd said.

She turned with two cups of coffee in hand and strolled over with that liquid grace of hers on full display. What she did with a pale silk blouse, black pencil skirt and kitten heels must've been illegal in some states. Surely a female couldn't get away with going around packing concealed weapons like those – broad shoulders, full breasts, narrow waist and swell of swell hips – not without landing in the clink somewhere or other, anyway. Just those long muscular legs alone, hiding under the innocuous black fabric, could get a strip joint closed down for obscenity.

But there was nothing obscene about this beauty. Not a damn thing. Angels can wear anything they please, and look any way they like. Michelangelo used to draw them stark naked, just not this sinfully lovely.

Suddenly we were in my inner office and the desk I was behind was my own, the spareness of the room broken only by a few framed wall photos of the occasional illustrious client, an operator's license, and a sharp-shooter award here and there. She sat with half of her hips slung on the edge of my desk and handed me the cup of coffee.

"Hope that's enough sugar and cream," Velda said, as if she hadn't made the mix a thousand times. "I know what a big sissy you are."

"Don't spoil me," I said, "right when you're cutting me loose."

She looked down on me. Even seated, she was tall. "I'm not cutting you loose. This is just for now."

"We could hire somebody to stay with your sister," I said. I sipped. Her coffee was always perfect. "I'm willing to pay the freight."

That babe could frown without creasing a damn thing. "It's not just Mikki, though I'd hate to think what I might've got myself into, the way kids have a mind of their own these days. It's Mom. That broken hip is going to take time to heal."

"Too much time. Doll, we can spend weekends out there in your mom's place. I got nothing against her moving to Long Island. It's... nice."

Velda shrugged and a scythe blade of black hair swung. "Maybe it'll come to that, Mike. For now, I want to be there for Mom and for Mikki. Surely you can understand."

"I'm a selfish only child. I don't understand shit."

She sipped her coffee. "I'm well aware you have a... flaw or two."

"Name one."

She laughed and, goddamnit, so did I.

"As long as Mom is in that nursing home," Velda said, "I should probably be there. Not that I'm really worried about Mikki."

"Naw, your sis is a good kid." Straight A student and budding tennis star that she was. "And I doubt your mom will put up with not being home for very long, either. Doll, you know I support you in anything you need to do. Family comes first."

Velda came around and sat in my lap and my swivel chair took it well, its groan almost like a purr. Arms around my neck, she planted a big sticky kiss on her big ugly boss and, when the clinch was over, lifted my chin with a red-nailed fingertip and said, "That's gonna have to hold you."

"Is this that cruel and unusual punishment I hear so much about?"

A shake of her head made the ebony arcs swing. "It's just the bitter truth. Can you handle it?"

"Haven't you heard? I'm a tough guy."

She gave me one more quick kiss. "You're an old softie."

"Where you're concerned, I am."

"We'll see each other weekends."

But we'd missed the last few. Work had kept me away, including the Ray Giles business for the *News*.

I watched her hip sway out from my inner office to her outer one, and it seemed a little exaggerated, trying too hard, taunting me, and then she closed the door behind her and I woke up.

I didn't even remember falling asleep on the reception-area couch. But I had. I sat on the edge of the thing and rubbed my eyes with the heels of my hands. I didn't remember taking off my porkpie hat and trench coat, but there they were, hanging on the coat tree near the door like the skin a snake crawled out of.

There had been that one, long, terrible period... almost seven years... when she'd been secretly called back to duty by the spooks and wound up behind the Iron Curtain on a mission the details of which still hadn't been wholly shared with me. Abandoned, I behaved like a punk, taking down a few peripheral bad guys, then crawling into one bottle after another.

But Velda came back to me, like no time at all had gone between, and I straightened the hell out and, since then, we had rarely been separated for long. We lived in the same apartment building, not together but "almost" married. She'd spent six months away, some years ago, when her aunt was very ill and needed care. I'd been miserable, not having her around – mail piled up and the office went to crap and I almost got myself killed doing P.I. work without her backing me up.

Fuck it.

On the spur of the moment, I decided: I would close up shop and join her on Long Island. I called Pat and told him.

"Good for you," Pat said. "You could use an attitude adjustment."

"I'll let Nat Drutman know I'm taking an open-ended leave of absence," I said. Nat owned and managed the Hackard Building. "And I'll send my referrals to the Smith-Torrence Agency, who've covered for me before."

"This sounds serious. You're not going to retire on me, are you, Mike?"

"Make up your mind, Pat. You want my attitude adjusted or me to stick around and keep doing your job for you?"

That I delivered lightly, much as the curse he answered it with was.

Then he said, a tiny edge in his voice, "Try not to get in any trouble on Long Island. You have a history there."

"That was a long time ago, Pat."

"Everything was a long time ago for us, buddy."

He clicked off.

At my apartment I packed a bag and in the parking garage collected the heap, as I referred to my nondescript black Ford with its souped-up engine. It wasn't the first heap. I bought a used patrol car every five years or so at a police auction, and the practice had stood me well. I considered giving Velda a call, but on the off-chance she might try to talk me out of coming, I just headed out.

The destination was Sidon, eighty miles out on Long Island, a tourist destination, though its off-season population was up to a year-round twenty thousand now. I did, as Pat indicated, have a history in the hamlet, having removed a crooked police chief and cleaned out a crooked gambling casino. Just a couple little side trips on a getaway meant for me to dry out and cool down after the personal trauma of who the killer of my army buddy Jack Williams turned out to be.

I'd thought Charlotte was the love of my life, but I'd been wrong. The love of my life was the ex-policewoman who did the filing and the typing and took client notes in shorthand and who went undercover for her boss, risking her pretty tail for me. Here I'd thought Charlotte, the blonde goddess who turned out to be a black widow, was the tragedy that wrecked my life... when there Velda was, the miracle that saved me.

The Sterling house was in the Sunrise Hills addition on the northern edge of Sidon, modest bungalows about half of which were summer homes, shuttered now. In the middle of just another nondescript block, facing more small ranch styles, the place boasted a modest, well-trimmed lawn and shrubbery that hugged four brick stairs to a cement landing that was less than a porch.

I pulled up in front, behind a gleaming gold Corvette, a late model looking like a mirage in a middle-class neighborhood like this. I frowned as I got out, leaving my bag in my buggy's back seat. I had a hunch I knew who that expensive ride belonged to, and it wasn't Velda or anyone else living in this only slightly overgrown cottage.

I didn't knock. The door was open and I went in, and somehow was not surprised when I moved through the humble living room with its old lady knickknacks and furnishings covered in plastic and on past the kitchen and into the little hallway that fed the three bedrooms. I peeked in at what I knew would be Velda's, a hunch confirmed by her suitcase, emptied on a stand, and a vanity with her make-up arrayed like soldiers ready to do battle. As for Mrs. Sterling's bedroom, its frilly drapes and air-freshener scent announced itself. Finally, I peeked into the guest room.

A teenage girl's bedroom, really – color "Let It Be" Beatles and black-and-white Robert Redford posters, pink walls, made bed with blue spread, portable record player on a stand.

And a girl – asleep on the bed in her wispy pink bra and panties – who didn't stir. Also a boy, with maybe a couple years on her, seventeen or eighteen, sitting up, startled; well-tanned, lithely muscular, blond and blue-eyed and handsome in a beach boy kind of way, he at least didn't have the usual long hair. A nice close-to-the- scalp trim. You had to like that much about him.

I curled my finger, summoning him, and – wide-eyed – he obeyed. I held the bedroom door open for him and, as at ease with himself in his skivvies as a nudist at a nudist colony, he padded out into the hall, leaving the slumbering Mikki unaware.

I am not proud of the fact that Mikki, with her long legs and full figure, reminded me startlingly of her older sister; but at least nothing stirred in me that wasn't anger. Well, irritation. She was on the too slender side, despite the Velda-ish bustiness – so many of these high school girls wanted to picture themselves as skinny fashion models nowadays.

I deposited the boy on the couch (a rare piece here of fifties vintage furniture that wasn't plastic-wrapped) facing the color TV I'd bought Mrs. Sterling two Christmases ago. I found a chair and dragged it over and sat and faced him.

I asked him, cheerfully, "Any reason why I shouldn't kick your ass?"

His voice was husky, mid-range. "You're Mike Hammer."

"That's right."

"Mikki's uncle."

"In name only, but yes."

He nodded, once. "I know about you. I *do* know about you. You're in the papers sometimes."

"Not so much lately, but yeah. What's that got to do with the price of tea in Harlem?"

He swallowed. "You could, at that."

"I could what?"

"Kick my ass. I'm not into sports or anything."

I jerked a thumb toward the street. "I figured that from the Vette. But you're 'into' *something*, aren't you?"

His eyes, which were light blue, widened again. "Mr. Hammer, I'm, uh, a friend of Mikki's."

"A good friend, I'd say."

Several nods now. "We're going together, yes. Not for long, but... yes. I never imagined anybody would catch us."

"Criminals never do."

His chin crinkled. "Is loving somebody a crime?"

I sighed. "Kid, I'm no saint, but—"

He sat forward, hands together, fingers intertwined. "Mr. Hammer, Mikki's sister is never around this time of day. She spends most afternoons with Mikki's mother, at the nursing home. I would never be so reckless as to... I mean... I wouldn't think of... well."

I stood. My turn to sigh. "Let's step outside."

The blue eyes popped in alarm. "Are you *going* to?"

"Am I going to what?"

"Kuh-kick my ass?"

I managed not to smile, stifling a laugh. "Outside, son. I don't want to wake your girl. Apparently she needs her rest after your... workout."

The boy blushed. He goddamn blushed! And I did laugh, once. "Put your clothes on," I said. "Quietly."

I followed him to where Mikki was still dead to the world. He got into a light blue Key West FLA tank top and chino shorts and sandals. I gave him an "after you" gesture and he headed back into the hall with me behind him like the arresting officer. Soon we were sitting on the edge of the stoop atop the steps.

"You're the Garrett kid," I said, "aren't you?"

He nodded. "Garrett Andrew Williams the Second. But everybody calls me 'Second.'"

"College boy?"

"Sophomore. Long Island University."

I'd heard Mikki speak of this scion of a wealthy family whose generations of money were strictly Wall Street. He had been popular, well-liked, the president of the senior class, a year or two ahead of her. What I hadn't known was that she was going with him – I knew of another guy, far less well-connected, who she'd been seeing, a kid who did not have this kind of pedigree. That must've been over. Or else this was a hell of an interruption.

"Listen, Second," I said, "I know boys will be boys and girls will be girls, particularly when the boy has a Corvette. But there are plenty of places on Long Island where you can park a vehicle and get busy in the back seat. Of course, a Vette doesn't *have* a back seat, but there are other, better options than a bedroom at her mother's house."

He was studying me. "You're not really... pissed at me?"

I waved that off. "I'm not that big a hypocrite. Jesus, son, this is a damn island – that makes for a lot of fucking beach. Grab some blankets and have a blast. But..."

I raised a forefinger.

"...use some damn precautions. You knock that girl up and we will re-negotiate that ass-kicking. Capeesh?"

"Capeesh," the boy said with a relieved grin.

"Now. Go home."

He nodded, got to his feet and then the gold Corvette was rocketing off. If he got a ticket, maybe it would underscore our little confrontation.

I was still seated there, thinking about how much times had changed, when I heard the screen door behind me creak open.

"Mike," my unofficial niece said. Her voice was spookily familiar.

She was a lovely thing, tall like Velda, and the jeans she'd tugged on had stylish worn holes and her terry-cloth top left her tummy bare, and how could you blame a healthy kid like Second?

Barefoot, toenails scarlet, she was wearing brown-tinted glasses, not sunglasses exactly, more a style thing, the lenses so big as to look silly in their tortoiseshell settings.

"I guess I'm not exactly the first female sinner," Mikki said, "you ever caught."

I patted the brick next to me. "It's not the sinning, it's the stupidity."

She plopped herself down. "I think my sister knows," she said, but uncertainly. "About Second, I mean."

"Maybe. But don't insult her. At least have the decency to sneak around."

That made her laugh a little, and then so did I.

"His hair is short," the girl said, in a peace-keeping sort of way. "Isn't that what counts with you?"

"I'm sure he's a nice kid. And he's rich. I like that about him."

The eyes behind those big tinted lenses were studying me. "Don't you want me to have to make my own way in the world?"

"I've tried that. It's overrated. Look, just be sensible."

Her eyebrows hiked above the big lenses. "Like Mike Hammer?"

"No! Hell no. Use precautions, and I recommend using, you know, not just the pill, but... go old-school."

"Rubbers you mean?"

Now I was the one blushing. "Hey, I lost the sexual revolution a long time ago. I can't keep up with you kids. But look, honey – just because he's cute and rich, that doesn't mean he's... forever."

She touched my nearest hand. "It kind of feels like it."

"It always does. Particularly at your age."

A car pulled up, a little green Mustang, settling in right behind the heap. Velda, in a brown one-piece velour pants suit that was designed to be nothing special but that she turned into something spectacular, got out, endless long legs first.

"What are you doing here?" she asked me, surprised but not quite cross. "It isn't the weekend."

"I heard there's a good burger joint in Sidon," I said. "Figured I'd check it out. Anybody interested?"

Soon we all were seated in Chuck's Burger Haven in downtown Sidon with malts and fries and burgers, and a ton of in-the-know locals. When Mikki went off to the restroom, my secretary and I had a quiet confab.

Velda said, "I'm a licensed investigator, you know."

"So I hear," I said. "So what?"

"So I saw the bag in the back seat. That's not the overnight number. That's the one you take on a plane."

"I didn't take a plane here. I drove."

"You came to stay a while," she said, one eyebrow arched, half a smile going.

"You *are* a detective."

"I'm not against it, you visiting," she admitted. "By my tally, following your bloody trail in the *News*, you've been in two shoot-outs since I came out here and you've shot, and killed, five bad guys."

"It was slow without you around."

A sigh, a shake of the head, black arcs swaying. "I remember the first getaway you made to Sidon. It was… memorable."

"Yeah. I remember. Saved you from a psychopath, as I recall."

She cocked her head. "Let's make this one a little more low-key. What say?"

Mikki was back. She slid into the booth on her sister's side.

"I say," I said, "it's good to see both of you girls. And nice to have a quiet getaway for once."

"I wonder," Velda said.

CHAPTER THREE

When we got back from the burger joint, the sun hadn't gone all the way down but was thinking about it. Velda and her sister went on in and I was fetching my bag from the heap, having transferred it to the trunk before we all piled in to go have a bite, when a motorcycle roared up sounding like the Hell's Angels rolling into town.

The big Harley bumped up over the curb and across the sidewalk and caught the edge of the lawn, taking some green with it. The engine switched off.

"Hey!" I yelled. Then in classic old man fashion added: "Get that fucking thing off the lawn, you damn jerk!"

The jerk in question was lanky in a much-worn black-leather vest over a long-sleeve tee, frayed blue jeans and motorcycle boots, no helmet over a head of dark hair held back in a ponytail, his boyish, admittedly handsome face stubbled with maybe a week of beard. Hooded eyes gave him a naturally sullen look, but he didn't argue with me, just guided the bike back onto the sidewalk, used the kickstand and walked quickly over. I was at the edge of the brick walk to the bungalow, the bag in hand, with half a mind to swing it at him.

"Sorry," the kid said, voice mid-range. He was maybe twenty; like Second, a little older than Mikki's high school crowd. "I was in a mood."

"Really?" I said, not holding back the nasty. "I get that way myself, when somebody tears up a lawn. Try planting the stuff and mowing it and you'll get what I mean."

He risked a tiny smile. "You must be Mr. Hammer. Mikki told me about you."

"She never told me about you, but I heard things."

He thought about that for a few moments, then extended his black-gloved hand. "I'm a friend of hers. Brian Ellis. You sure she never mentioned me?"

I shook the hand; the grip was firm, anyway. "I'd remember. What can I do for you? Or were you just leaving?"

"I just stopped by to see how Mikki's mother is doing."

Was I supposed to believe that?

He went on: "You mind if I go up to the house? I wanna talk to her."

"Mikki's mother is in a nursing home."

"I mean, I want to talk to Mikki." He raised a gloved palm. "Sorry we got off on the wrong foot, Mr. Hammer."

"How is it you know me? Can't just be Mikki talking."

"I saw you in the paper a few times."

What was I, a damn comic strip?

"You killed five men, it said, last few weeks," he commented. He seemed impressed and maybe a bit more intimidated than most bikers would be of some old guy who told 'em to get off his lawn.

"It was two different times," I said, a little defensive, though not exactly knowing why. "The papers like to make a big deal out of everything."

"You... you mind if I ask you something?"

"Try it and see."

His eyes, gray-blue, narrowed. "How... how does it feel to kill somebody?"

I grunted something that was more or less a laugh. "I'd tell you to ask your psychology teacher, but I'm guessing you're not in high school like Mikki."

"Uh, no. I... was. But I *am* in college. Now."

I almost said, *You're shitting me*, but I had too much class, college or otherwise. "Then maybe ask your psyche prof... or do you want a personal answer?"

His chin came up. "I'm asking 'cause I want to know. I don't mean any offense by it."

I shrugged. "It depends on the situation, killing a man. If it's war, it's not about the enemy's bad luck but your own ass. Why isn't a healthy guy like you in Vietnam, anyway?"

"I'm 4-F."

"Yeah? Lucky you."

Now he risked a frown. "Not so lucky. I lost my left arm when I skidded in front of a four-wheeler."

I hadn't noticed it, but his left arm did hang loose at his side. Probably a prosthesis. I felt bad for being so tough on the kid.

But it didn't stop me from saying, "If that's all you got, out of a dust-up with a four-wheeler, you *are* lucky." I sighed. "If you want to know how I felt about those drug dealers I took down, truth is? I didn't feel a goddamn thing."

"No... no remorse at all?"

"When somebody's shooting at you, and you return fire? Remorse isn't part of it. Strictly survival. You ever been shot at?"

"Of course not."

"Try it sometime."

"*Brian!*" Mikki's voice called.

Mikki, still in her terry-cloth top and distressed jeans, came quickly out and down the steps on low-heeled sandals, pausing to whisper to me, "I'll deal with this."

Then the girl was shaking a finger in the Ellis kid's face and reaming him a good one, although I didn't catch anything of what she said, as her voice was down and I was heading into the house with my bag.

I met Velda at the door.

She gave me a look, the big brown eyes narrow. "Old boyfriends," Velda said. "Always a problem."

I went in and set my bag down. "Like when I pulled you out of that undercover operation with that pimp I wound up shooting?"

"Maybe not *that* big a problem." She gave me a kiss, a quick one. "Let them talk it out."

From the muffled arguing through the closed door, mostly Mikki's voice, I'd say "talking it out" was an understatement.

But I said, "Sure."

We were at the front window now, keeping an eye on things — with a rough kid like Ellis, who knew where this might lead? But then the brouhaha ended with the easy rider roaring off and, right on cue, Second pulled up in his golden Corvette.

Dressed as before, he got out, clearly concerned, went to her quickly and put his hands on her shoulders. Mikki seemed to be assuring him everything was fine.

What guy doesn't flip out a little when his girl's ex-boyfriend comes around? We were all lucky the three of them weren't there at the same time, or things could've really got out of hand.

We saw Mikki nod at Second, leaving him at the curb as she came trotting toward the house; we pulled back from the window, not wanting to seem like we were minding her business and not our own, and the girl stuck her head in the door.

"Second is here," Mikki said redundantly. "We're going to catch a drive-in movie. *Woodstock*'s playing."

Then she slipped out.

I said, "I don't think that one has much of a plot."

"Isn't that the bird in *Peanuts*?"

"Who knows? I'm still a *Terry and the Pirates* man myself."

Velda smirked at me. "You just have a yen for Dragon Lady types."

"I sure do."

That made her smile. "Let's get you settled in, sonny boy, before you widen the generation gap any further."

We went to the guest bedroom, where Velda was already camped out, and I set my bag on top of the bureau and filled the bottom two drawers. I'd just completed the task when I heard a long zipper humming its way down and reacted like a hound who clocked its master digging into a box of doggie treats.

Her brown velour pants suit puddled at her feet. She stepped out of them, wearing a beige support bra and matching panties that weren't at all sexy but for their remarkable contents. She kicked off the dark brown kitten heels and undid the bra and it hung there a while, like mountain climbers who missed a step, then fell away; she shimmied out of the panties and a pubic tuft sprang into view and said hello.

Then she was standing there, hands defiantly on her hips, the full breasts with their hard pink tips thrust forward in dual dares, the muscular legs planted apart, like the statue of some ancient Amazon, a warrior queen whose shameless confidence knew no bounds.

By way of comparison, my strip tease was nothing to write home about, more like a kid on a hot day shedding his duds to jump in a lake and get cooled off, only there was nothing cool about what followed. Unlike the horny teens I'd interrupted earlier, we got under the covers and had some good old-fashioned frantic missionary sex, the kind called for when you haven't seen your partner in weeks.

Why had I waited so many years to partake of her sweet fruit? It had taken those seven years apart for me to toss off my silly ideas about respecting convention, to believe that flings were fine but not with that special someone. Only now that we were truly partners, marriage license or not, all of that was irrelevant. Not long ago, on a hillside, with a dead miscreant named Blackie Conley at its foot, in the heat of surviving an assault, we had tossed off everything from clothes to customs and finally merged as man and wife. We'd wed for society one day; for now and forever, we already were.

Velda padded off into the hall bathroom and I got a smoke out of the breast pocket of my discarded shirt. Pulled on my boxers just to be decent and crawled back under the covers and lit up a Lucky.

She came in nude as a grape and slipped under with me. "Smoking after sex? You are such a cliche."

"I never claimed not to be."

She plucked it from my fingers like a flower, got out of bed again and disappeared bare-ass. I heard a toilet flush.

Under the covers again, pretending to be cranky, Velda said, "How many times have you quit?"

"Counting right now? Half a dozen maybe. You know me. I get weak when I get traumatized."

"Why are you traumatized?"

"My best girl ran out on me."

My Viking woman touched my face; the long red fingernails tickled. "Well, your best girl's right here, right now. So no more bad habits."

"Take my bad habits away, doll, and what do you have left?"

Her smile turned nicely wicked. "Maybe somebody who'll finally make an honest woman of me."

She pressed against me and nuzzled under my ear, the long black hair providing a second round of tickling. Then with her sweet face in the nape of my neck, my loyal secretary fell asleep and so did I.

When I awoke, and sat up a bit, not remembering where I was for a moment, she woke, too. Nothing but night was coming in around the window by the bureau. A clock on my nightstand read a luminous ten after ten. Velda reached over toward her bedside lamp and turned on a light at a low level.

She bent and opened her nightstand drawer and withdrew a pack of Virginia Slims and a silver horse's-head lighter I'd given her years ago. After selecting a slender smoke from the pack, and lighting herself up, she offered me one.

I grinned at her. "When did you become a hypocrite?"

"A long time ago. I had a good teacher." She nodded at me, encouragingly, offering the tobacco deck my way. "Take one – it probably won't turn you gay."

"What the hell," I said with a bare-shouldered shrug, "I'll risk it."

She lit me up and, with a devilish smile, said, "You've come a long way, baby."

We smoked in silence for a while, our exhales drifting like our thoughts. As a cigarette, this was better than nothing.

"What's the deal?" I asked her.

"What do you mean, what's the deal?"

"You haven't smoked for years. Or have you been sneaking them behind my back?"

She cocked her head. "Nobody can sneak anything behind Mike Hammer's back. You're the most famous detective in Manhattan, remember?"

"Maybe, but we're in Sidon." I let some smoke out. "Has it got you down, baby, your mother's condition?"

"No, she's doing well. Making progress, healing on schedule. Of course, it's anything but immediate."

I studied her. "Then what's got you filling your lungs with the Surgeon General's warning?"

She had a troubled look now. "It's our... it's my sister."

"Mikki? She seems fine to me."

"It feels like… I'm probably wrong." She let smoke out her nostrils, a lovely Dragon Lady. "It's just the difference in our ages, Mikki and me."

"What is?"

She turned to me, her eyes narrowed. "You know how important tennis has been to her."

I shrugged. "Sure. She's getting more college scholarship offers than the entire Jericho High basketball team. She's gonna be the next Billie Jean King."

Her head shook slowly. "Not if she doesn't go out for tennis this year, she won't."

That sat me up. "What? I thought tennis was just about the most important thing in her life."

"No, Mike, she's a normal girl of seventeen. Lately she's been majoring in Boys."

That got a frown out of me. "You can't mean she's turning into some kind of little…" I couldn't get the word "slut" out, but Velda knew it was on the tip of my tongue.

Her reply was firm. "No. Not at all. She went with this older boy for a while, the one you saw outside…"

"The Ellis kid."

"Yes. I wasn't crazy about that, nor was Mom. Some biker boy from a broken home. But he was always polite to me. You can't judge a book by its cover, they say."

"Well, they're wrong. Ever see what they put on the front of *The Carpetbaggers*? That kid is a classic bad boy, from his motorcycle to his boots to that long, greasy hair."

That seemed to amuse her a little. "Some females are attracted to 'bad boys,' Mike. Haven't you been paying attention?"

She had me there.

"Look," Velda said, "she's with Second now, and he's a good kid from a good family. Older than her, but in university. Let's not look a gift horse in the mouth."

"Maybe so, but..."

"But what, Mike?"

Reluctantly I told her about catching those two in Mikki's mom's bedroom, half-dressed, obviously in a post-coital state.

"The girl's a senior in high school," Velda said, placatingly. "Second's a sophomore in college. That she, that they, have an active sex life in today's world is no surprise. How old was I when we first got together?"

Truth was, I didn't remember asking.

"It probably has to do with her improved self-image," Velda said, thoughtfully.

"What's that supposed to mean? You listening to Dr. Joyce Brothers again?"

She shrugged her bare shoulders. "You know that Mikki put on some weight in her junior year."

"Yeah, some. Didn't slow her down on the tennis court."

"Not much, but how she felt about herself was impacted, and she really worked at losing weight. She's darn near skinny now."

"Maybe a little. But she looked fine to me."

"She looks fine. But there's a downside."

"Oh?"

Velda leaned on an elbow. "Most obviously, it's her not going out for tennis, no matter how much her coach encourages her. Doesn't mean a thing to her that her school counselor is talking all these scholarship offers, if she just stays at it. Of course, that might be a moot point."

"Why's that?"

Her head cocked. "Frankly, Mike, I wasn't aware of this. Mom tried to keep it from me while she worked on... the problem."

"*What* problem?"

She made a face, then: "Mikki's grades."

I waved that off. "Oh, come on. She's been a straight A student since elementary school."

But Velda shook her head and the raven arcs seemed to swing in slow motion. "Last semester she barely managed a C- average. She's getting Ds now."

I frowned. "Did you know about this?"

"No, not for a long time. As I said, my mother thought she could deal with it herself. But that was before Mom broke her hip and wound up in a nursing home."

"Which is why you took your leave of absence."

Velda nodded. "Which is why I took my leave of absence. *Somebody* has to look after that child."

My smirk had no humor in it. "A child who has a boyfriend she makes hay with when the cat's away."

"Now who's the hypocrite?"

"No, no, it's fine. And if she wants to marry that rich kid and clip investment coupons and raise a bunch of spoiled brats to make Ivy League legacy students out of, that's up to her. I guess. I was kind of looking forward to her winning the U.S. Open someday."

Velda's sigh was knowing. "Kids go their own way, Mike. If you were a father, you'd know that."

"I already know it. But I don't have to like it. And Mikki's my goddaughter, remember."

She gestured with an open palm. "Mikki breaking off with the Ellis boy is a good sign. Personally, I thought Brian was a nice kid, a little misguided maybe, but… just the same, Second is much better for her. Great family, nice prospects…"

"And short hair," I said.

She laughed. "Yes, I know how important that is to you."

We drifted back off to sleep, and something in the outer room woke me. I sat up sharply, taking in the luminous dial on my nightstand clock: well past two a.m.!

The lovely naked woman next to me roused as well, and said, whispering, "It's not the bad guys, Mike. That's just Mikki coming in. This is Long Island."

"I know it is," I said defensively. But my hand was in my nightstand drawer, where I'd stowed the .45. "But I have 'friends' in Manhattan who get around."

Some muffled laughter and talk out there, followed by the door closing and footsteps in the hall, announced Velda's reading of the situation as spot on. The only surprise was the quick knock at the guest-room door followed by that door opening.

No light was on in the hall, but the shadowed form was clearly female.

Not every woman in the world is my friend, so I turned the .45 in hand toward that open doorway and a hand reached in and clicked on the light. The "woman" poised there was Mikki, looking a little rumpled, both hair and clothing, but smiling big.

"Don't shoot!" she said, holding up her hands, giggling.

I snapped, "Do you know what time it is, young lady?"

"What's that?" Mikki said, still amused, taking in our half-concealed nude forms under a sheet. "Naked indignation...? Good night, you two. Nice to see you, Mike. Even if I'm seeing more than I care to."

The girl clicked off the light and went out, shutting the door.

Velda clicked on her nightstand light. She seemed amused, too.

"I don't find that funny," I said, cross.

"It *is* kind of funny."

"Didn't you see what *time* it is?"

Her chin lowered and her eyes came up. "We both saw. It was a drive-in movie. They're always at least double features, and this isn't that late for that. Hey, she's just pushing things because Mom is not around, and this is Spring Break, and she's a senior, and—"

"Okay, okay," I said, and slipped the rod back in the nightstand drawer. "I'll cut her some slack."

"Good. And maybe she'll cut you some."

Velda switched off the nightstand lamp.

CHAPTER FOUR

The Sidon Country Club's winding front entrance led to a clubhouse that might have been an old estate, two white stucco stories with one-story extensions on either side wearing three red-tiled roofs like jaunty, if sun-bleached, hats. I left the heap in a parking lot offering more spaces than necessary this time of year, and Velda and I entered through double doors into an oldish foyer in a facility apparently last modernized during FDR's first term.

We moved past framed golf photos and a trophy case on either side of some fresh flowers on a table and on through a featureless dining room that was showing its age by its worn red carpet if nothing else. At just after eleven, a handful of diners seemed spotted around as if to keep the place looking honest. The Sidon Country Club had seen better days, but was holding its own in an age when its time-honored shallow values were in question.

No host or hostess stopped us from making our way through to a terrace with an expansive view of the greening course beyond the pool, though neither swimming nor golf – which spelled backward is "flog," by the way – were in demand about now. The 19th Hole bar, however, all dark wood, red trimmings and drifting cigarette smoke, was doing good business, tables of middle-aged men ridiculous in sideburns and mustaches and bushy hair, all decked out in Nehru jackets, turtlenecks, and bellbottoms.

"Good God," I said, barely loud enough for even me to hear, "how have I lived long enough to see this?"

Velda, at my side, curvaceous in an orange corduroy jumpsuit, whispered, "Mike, you are just not with it."

"I'd have to be in a coma," I said, "to let my sideburns grow out like that."

Her laughter was like gentle water falling from a high fountain. "I'll keep the barbers away while you're napping."

At the bar, a red-jacketed bartender around the age of his clientele and wearing the same style of sideburns and mustache, but bald, had the look of a GI who'd barely survived the Big One only to come home to a small postwar. He asked us what we'd have, and I said just some answers to a couple of questions, thanks. I made this point with an engraving of Abe Lincoln.

He or nobody checked to see if we were members, but maybe that would be bad form. Any bar would be glad to have Velda in it, and I was about as respectably casual as Mike Hammer gets in my tan sports coat and black polo shirt and lighter tan chinos.

Mid-morning, Mikki had gone off with Second to a pool party at the young man's parents' palatial place. I had questions that Velda couldn't answer, so we'd set about to satisfy my native curiosity. Velda called the high school, operating strictly skeleton crew during Spring Break, only to be told information about the teaching staff was confidential. By announcing her status as the sister of a student, however, Vel managed to learn that tennis coach Mark Traynor worked part-time at the country club, giving lessons. He might be there catching a few extra hours.

The bartender confirmed that and gave us directions – "Just a quick walk to the east" – to the twin tennis courts, which were covered by a fabric air dome.

We found the trimly brown-haired, muscularly slender, boyishly handsome Traynor training (appropriately enough) an attractive blonde pupil of perhaps forty in what might have been nurse's whites, had the medical profession allowed short sleeves, short shorts, and sneakers. Traynor wore a Sidon Senior High sweatshirt ("Go Gophers!") and navy shorts and, of course, trainers.

Standing close behind her, the instructor guided the student's racket-wielding arm with care as she looked back at him gratefully for providing a little warmth – the place was heated to a degree, but not enough so to matter on a crisp spring day like this.

Velda and I traded raised-eyebrow glances and took a white-slatted bench adjacent to the court and waited our turn. The lesson continued – balls were in play, let's say – and after fifteen minutes, the blonde, who had a fine gleaming sweat going, pressed a hand around her trainer's, chatted briefly and thanked him ever so, then trotted off the court to another bench, where she gathered a towel, slung it around her shoulders and, racquet in hand, bounced into the great outdoors like a foul ball worth snagging.

"She has nice form," Velda said archly.

"I hadn't noticed," I lied.

Traynor grabbed a towel from the same bench as his departed student, rubbed his face, slung it around his neck, and came over to us with a friendly if guarded smile.

"I'm afraid," he said, "these are private lessons."

I'll bet, I thought.

He continued: "By which I mean, unless you're family or something... and I don't recognize you folks... it's really best we not have spectators."

I'll bet, Velda must've thought.

We stood.

I said, "We *are* family, but not that country club gal's – this is Velda Sterling, Mikki's big sister. I'm the girl's godfather. Mike Hammer."

His head went back a little and his eyes narrowed. "Ooooh... I heard you were Mikki's 'uncle,' Mr. Hammer. You're quite a well-known character in this part of the world."

Velda said, "He's quite a character whatever part of the world he's in."

Traynor laughed lightly. "Well, I don't have a lesson scheduled for another half hour. Might I assume you're here to talk about Mikki?"

"You might," I said.

"Shall we go into the bar?" he asked, eyes going from Velda to me. "We can have something to drink and talk. I think it's worth doing."

"Drinking?" Velda asked. "Or talking?"

He didn't respond to that, other than with a little laugh, and then led us toward the clubhouse.

"Don't get the wrong idea about that private lesson," Traynor said, with a slightly abashed smile. "Mrs. Daigle, that's my student you saw, is an enthusiastic woman. She likes to be friendly and I let her. That was a fifty-dollar bill she handed me before she flounced off."

I wondered what a C-note got her.

We didn't need to get on this guy's bad side, so I said, "I understand. Velda here is my secretary-slash-fiancée, and she gets her nose out of joint when I get too friendly with my female clients."

She slapped my arm gently. "Do I, now?"

I raised my eyebrows at him and he smiled, and everything was cool.

In the 19th Hole, we took a booth toward the back. No waitress was working, so Traynor and I collected our drinks at the bar – he had an orange juice and I got Velda and me two ginger ales – and went back and settled in.

"On Long Island," he said, still somewhat apologetic about the flirtation we'd witnessed, "a teacher's salary doesn't stretch very far. Coaching tennis and swim team, with my Driver's Ed classes, all adds up to a passable income, but I have to moonlight to make it. This country club gig really helps out. I've got a young wife and a two-year-old to support, you know."

I didn't know. But what I did know was that a guy can have a wife and kid and still fool around. I rarely did divorce work, but plenty has been offered my way.

He sported a nice white smile as boyish as the rest of him. "Velda... may I call you that, Ms. Sterling?"

"Please."

He leaned across the table a little. His expression seemed earnest. "I'm glad to have a chance to talk to you about Mikki. I understand your mother is hospitalized right now."

Velda nodded. "Mom broke her hip. She's in a nursing home here on the Island."

"Sorry to hear about her injury... but I'm happy to talk to you, because you might have insights about your sister that an older woman, like your mom, might not."

We were here to get insights out of him, not the other way around. But I let that ride for now. I sipped my ginger ale.

"I guess I don't have to tell you, Velda," he said, his serious expression taking some of the boyish handsomeness out of his face, "that your sister's had scholarship offers from some of the best colleges, with the top tennis programs, in the country."

Velda nodded. "I am aware of that."

He grunted a non-laugh. "Mikki's turning a blind eye to some incredible opportunities. As a sophomore and junior, she looked like she was on her way to a good college program and then the pros. Women's tennis has really taken hold, lots of TV interest, and she had a bright future in her pocket."

"*Had*, you say," I said.

He sighed. "Well, her game has been off this year. Not disastrously so, and at first I ascribed it to the pressure she's been under, the eyes that someone with her potential can have on her. But this spring season has been very disappointing to Mikki, I know. And I've been tough on her. Still, not near enough so for her to simply up and quit, the way she has."

Velda said, "You don't strike me as an unforgiving coach."

"Tennis just isn't that kind of sport – particularly women's tennis. We have our showboat male players with foul tempers, like this kid Jimmy Connors coming up. But it's kind of a, well, frankly, country club sport. It's not like the coaches ream the players the way, say, football coaches do."

How do *they "ream" them*, I wondered.

"Her grades are off, too," Velda said.

"So I understand," Traynor said, nodding. "Velda, if I might ask… do you know of Mikki taking any weight loss drugs? Diet pills? Amphetamines, barbiturates…?"

"No," Velda said. "But I know Mikki was concerned that she was getting overweight."

"Yes," the coach said, "and she expressed that to me as well. Felt her weight was limiting her game, affecting her play… and if she *was* taking dangerous weight-control drugs, with their possibility of mood altering, and it led to her quitting the sport she loved so much… what a bitter, ironic outcome that would be."

"So she lost interest in sports," Velda said, "and in academics… we *are* talking about a teenage girl, here. Couldn't just it be boy trouble?"

Traynor thought about that for a while, sipped his orange juice, then said, "I hesitate to get into that… but boy trouble *could* be the problem. I did see evidence of it."

I asked, "How so?"

He wasn't meeting our eyes now, as if his quietly expressed words were personal thoughts. "Mr. Hammer…"

"'Mike' is fine."

"Mike. Mikki and I got close – tennis is a hands-on sport."

"I noticed," I said, and Velda nudged me under the table.

Traynor went on: "And Mikki was my student in Driver's Ed, too – I was with her when she tested for, and got, her license. So she wasn't just… another student. She was special. So bright, such a terrific natural athlete. But she was torn between…" He swallowed, glanced away. "I'm a little uncomfortable with this."

Velda asked, "Are you betraying a confidence?"

Now he turned his head to meet her gaze. "No, but... we're friends, Mikki and I, as much as any student and teacher can be."

"Go on," I said, a little tightly.

"She seemed to be... pulled between two young men. Attracted to both, pursued by both."

"Seemed?" Velda asked.

He shrugged a single shoulder. "Mikki's not in my range of influence now. Driver's Ed was last semester, and she dropped out of tennis weeks ago. Both those young men could be out of her life by now, as far as I know."

I said, "You're talking about that Ellis kid and the boy they call Second."

His nod came quick. "Yes, Mike – Brian Ellis and Garrett Andrew Williams the Second. His father owns this country club with some of his associates. Second's father, I mean."

"For a rich kid," I said, "Second seems to have his head screwed on straight."

"He does. He's a good kid. Top student, excellent in his first years of college, I understand. The Ellis boy is a little older, and not nearly so impressive. I believe he's going to college, too – Suffolk Junior, so maybe he *is* trying."

I asked, "What else can you tell me about this Ellis kid?"

Traynor shrugged again. "Just that, in high school, he was an underachiever. And something of a doper."

That sent my hackles rising. "A dealer?"

Traynor waved that off. "I don't think so. Just your garden-variety stoner. Lot of them around these days. Harmless."

I bristled. "Ask the kids strung out on H about that."

His expression was conciliatory. "Mr. Hammer, Mike, this gateway drug stuff is nonsense. I wish these kids would find a new hobby, but I don't think smoking a little grass is going to lead to bigger things, necessarily. I drank beer in high school and I'm not an alcoholic."

"So did I," I said, "and I am."

He finished his juice and rose. "I should get ready for my next lesson. I hope I've been of some help. Don't hesitate to let me know if there's anything else I can do to be of help."

He went quickly out while Velda and I lingered over our ginger ales.

I asked her, "You think maybe Mikki's favorite teacher put the make on her, and then she got out of Dodge, fast as her tennies could carry her?"

"Maybe," Velda said, thinking, looking into her glass of soda as if it might contain the answer. Then she looked up at me, the dark eyes narrowing. "But I felt her coach was being frank. Let's take him at face value till we know otherwise."

I took a last swig of the pop and scooted out of the booth. "Doll, I don't take anybody but you and me at face value."

The Sidon Nursing and Rehab Center was a low-slung one-story pink stucco affair that might have been a ranch-style house got out of hand. The front of the facility had plenty of windows nearly as tall as the structure itself and a portico entrance leading to four glass doors – all very pleasant unless you were stuck here getting over something.

We left the heap in another underused parking lot and, in a

pale-pink-walled anonymously modern outer area, checked in at the front desk – it wasn't visiting hours per se, but Velda had no trouble getting us in to see Mrs. Mildred Sterling. Clustered around was a group of wheelchair-seated residents looking longingly at the windows and doors, as if planning to make a break for it. Nurses moved through with no such illusionary longings, younger friendlier ones stopping to chat with this patient or that one, the more seasoned staff oblivious, as if these weren't humans but potted plants.

As we walked the corridor, I said, "With any luck I'll get killed in a shoot-out before my life comes to this."

"Oh, it's not so bad. Anyway, your shoot-outs usually put others in the hospital."

I shrugged. "Or the morgue."

Just making conversation.

Velda's mom had a private room and, in a dark pink top and slacks seemingly designed to go with the place, looked comfy in a recliner with a pillow under her legs. She was your standard-issue little old lady with the ghost of youthful attractiveness remaining in her roundish face in its curly gray-haired setting. She was smaller than Velda and pudgy but not fat. But she obviously once had possessed the beauty she'd bequeathed to her daughter.

Mrs. Sterling beamed upon seeing us, of course, my presence a pleasant surprise – we'd always got along – and she was in the midst of dealing with a pleasant clipboard-bearing nurse while Velda and I dragged chairs over to wait our turn.

Acknowledging us with nods and smiles, the nurse departed and we pulled our chairs up, and small talk followed. I let Mrs. Sterling know I was staying on in Sidon for a while, my office temporarily shuttered; and Velda queried Mrs. Sterling about how they were treating her here and so on. Her mother seemed satisfied.

"It's pleasant enough," she said. "And the food is good, if on the starchy side. Just wish this place weren't so expensive."

"You're worth it, Mom," Velda said.

I asked, "How long will you be staying at this particular hotel?"

"At least another six weeks." Velda's mom had a musical voice, a second soprano and not her daughter's husky alto. "Be out of here by the start of summer, I should think."

"Mrs. Sterling," I said, "I'd like to get your take on Mikki and her troubling behavior lately – quitting tennis, her grades slipping, all of it."

Mrs. Sterling sighed. "I'm disappointed, of course. She might well have won a full ride scholarship, little budding tennis star that she was."

"Till now," Velda said.

Mrs. Sterling had Velda's dark eyes. "I'm hopeful Mikki will go to a college with a good tennis program, and just... what's the term?"

I said, "Walk on?"

She nodded. "Walk on and secure a spot on a team somewhere. Earn a place. Even some junior colleges have decent programs, you know, well within our means."

Velda said, "Before that could happen, her interest in the sport would have to be rekindled."

"It would. But Mikki's a young girl, and young girls make bad decisions all the time... *and* straighten out, all the time."

"She seems," I said, "like a nice kid, tennis or no tennis. Does she need to 'straighten out'? High school athletes sometimes lose interest in a sport where they've previously excelled. She may have seen what the collegiate competition is like, the advanced level of play, and had second thoughts."

"I think you're right on both accounts, Mike," Velda's mom admitted. "Mikki *is* a nice girl... but she's going through the kinds of pressures many girls her age go through – not eating enough because she wants to look like a model, running around with boys when she should be studying."

Velda said, "You wouldn't say she's... boy crazy, would you, Mom?"

Mrs. Sterling frowned, shook her head. "No. I do think she's been torn between those two *particular* boys – the nice young man from a good family, and... excuse me for putting so crudely... that trailer trash boy with the motorbike."

Velda turned to me. "Mikki was going with this Brian Ellis first, and fell in with his rough bunch. Then the two broke up and she started in with Second, and began running with a better crowd."

"It's all about cliques at her age," I said.

"At least that ruffian," Mrs. Sterling said, and it was an almost comic way to put it, "is out of her life now. He hung around the house all the time and I could hardly put up with it. I... I even caught them... I hate to admit it."

"Caught them how?" I asked.

Keeping her voice hushed, Velda's mom said, "She and this Brian... in bed together. In *her* bed, in *her* room. I'm afraid my little Mikki is no virgin."

We did not, of course, share with Mrs. Sterling the French farce Velda and I had performed for Mikki in the spare bedroom. Or the earlier one I'd interrupted with Mikki and Second.

"Times have changed," I admitted. "You call Ellis a 'ruffian' – why? Was he rude? We saw them arguing yesterday. Does he ever get violent with her, that you know of? If he laid a hand on that girl, I'll—"

Mrs. Sterling's eyebrows raised; for a moment she really looked like Velda. "He laid more than a 'hand' on her, but I don't think in *that* kind of way. I never saw him strike her or anything of that nature. It was just his… demeanor. You know, the way he dressed. The long hair. The crude way he talked, such filthy language. How he swaggered around."

I couldn't take that too seriously: I'd been accused of swagger myself. And the occasional fucking obscenity. Still, you hate to see that kind of thing going on around an impressionable young woman like Mikki.

"Such a bad influence," Mrs. Sterling said, her eyes – her whole face – tight. She was a jury foreman announcing a stiff sentence to a judge. But who was I to judge?

"Second, on the other hand," she said, smiling a little, almost wistful, "he's a breath of fresh air. Polite, well dressed. From a good family."

I flipped a hand. "Boys will be boys, Mrs. Sterling. All of that hasn't changed any of the facts: Mikki is still a quitter, taking herself off the tennis team that would've been her ticket out. And her grades are still terrible. Being with Second has hardly turned her around."

"Give it time," Mrs. Sterling said. "Bad influences always linger longer than good ones."

Velda said, "Well, the Ellis boy is still a lingering presence. Mikki's obviously tried to cut things off with him, but he doesn't seem to get it."

I said, "I'll talk to him."

Velda gave me a raised eyebrow look. "Mike…"

I raised a palm. "Just talk. I promise." I shifted in my chair. "Mrs. Sterling, you said the Ellis kid hung around your house a lot, while Mikki was going with him."

Her frown was grave. "Yes. He did. I didn't like it, but what's a mother to do?"

I asked, "Did you notice anything suspicious during the time Ellis was around?"

She didn't hesitate in her response. "I certainly did. A watch of mine, an expensive Rolex that Velda's late stepfather gave me, went missing. So did my wedding ring with a very nice, sizeable diamond. I'd stopped wearing it a few years ago. Didn't fit and I meant to get it re-sized but never got around to it."

Velda asked, "When did you notice this?"

"Just recently, but it could have happened any time. It may not have anything to do with anything."

I asked, "You suspect Ellis?"

Mrs. Sterling sighed. Shrugged. "I shouldn't accuse him. I have no specific reason to suspect him, other than… well."

"Well what?"

"I overheard him and Mikki arguing, and I wondered if it might be about the theft, if that's what it was. It may have been what broke them up and allowed the young Second boy to move in. It's a bit of a mystery. Be nice to get to the bottom of it."

"That, Mrs. Sterling," I said, "is where I come in."

CHAPTER FIVE

That evening, Mikki was about to go out to a dance with Second, and had yet to emerge from her bedroom, when the boy showed up. Garrett Andrew Williams the Second was dressed not unlike those middle-aged men at the country club – a gold paisley long-sleeve shirt and red bell bottoms – but on him it didn't look quite as ridiculous.

Not quite.

Standing there in the doorway, after I'd answered his bell, the blond, blue-eyed boy still seemed a little embarrassed seeing me, after my catching him in bed with Velda's sister.

"Evening, son," I said. "Stay out there."

He blinked at me, apprehensively, and I joined him on the porch, its light on, and left the door slightly ajar. I took him by the arm and walked him down the steps and onto the sidewalk. The gold Corvette at the curb seemed designed to go with his apparel, but I doubted even someone with a pedigree like Second's had multiple sports cars to go with his various wardrobe selections.

The evening was clear, stars already out, and a pleasant balmy breeze had replaced the earlier chill of the day in the Sunrise Hills addition after sunset. Lights were on in neighborhood homes and the world seemed like a safe, friendly place.

"I-I thought everything was cool between us, Mr. Hammer," the boy said. He was shaking a little.

I raised a calming palm. "This isn't about the other afternoon when we caught you two, uh, napping. As long as we have an understanding about you using precautions if you and Mikki get frisky."

Both his palms came up, more surrender than calming. "Absolutely. So, uh… what did you want to talk about? What time to be back with Mikki tonight? The South Hampton Ballroom's a good half hour from here, and—"

"That's not it, son," I said. "Like I said, guys of my generation are nobody to lecture yours on morality. I just want you to stay safe going about it."

His grin was relieved if nervous. "No problem, Mr. Hammer."

I stood close enough to him to rest a hand on his shoulder, and did. "What I want to ask you about… and I don't mean to pry… but how do you think Mikki is doing?"

He frowned in thought. "In what way?"

I removed the hand and gestured to myself. "From our point of view, her sister and me, we're concerned about any number of things."

He didn't seem to be following. "What sort of things?"

"Her weight loss. Her dropping out of tennis. Her near-failing grades. None of it is like her."

He sighed, smiled a little. "Mr. Hammer…"

"Why don't you call me 'Mike'? Just being around kids like you and Mikki makes me feel old enough already."

Minor traffic sounds, a few blocks over, provided a backdrop for our conversation. Somewhere a baby was crying; somewhere else a dog was barking.

Second laughed a little. "Okay, Mike." He took a beat and a breath. "I think she's doing okay. Lots of girls where we go to school are weight conscious. They all want to look like models or something."

"Guess they don't know guys like a little meat on the bone."

He chuckled. "Guess not. Mikki just wants to look nice. Surely there isn't anything wrong with that."

I gave him a hard look. "No. As long as she isn't using weight-control drugs to do it, or going all anorexic."

Second shook his head; his smile turned serious. "That's just not her. Mikki's not that kind of girl."

"She could be doing such things in private. If she's self-conscious about her weight, she's not likely to tell you."

He shrugged, a little confusion showing. "I suppose, maybe."

"But you might've noticed something. You need to do me, and her, and *yourself*, a favor. Keep aware of any signs. Read between the lines when you two talk. Could you do that for me, son?"

He frowned. "I hope you don't mean you want me to spy on her."

"Not asking that. Just keep an eye out. You know what business I'm in, right?"

"Sure. I know all about who you are, Mr. Hammer. Mike."

"Well, a good number of my clients in recent years have been the parents of runaways. The parents of girls who hadn't evidenced any major unhappiness, other than the usual behavior of a lot of kids – secrecy, sullenness. Good girls, fine students, cheerleaders, you name it – wholesome all the way. And then they disappear and when I finally find them they're junkies or prostitutes or porn queens or all of the above, and lost to their parents and the world."

Second was shaking his head. "Mike... that isn't Mikki. You *know* it isn't Mikki."

I shrugged. "I don't *think* it's her. You're right. But parents and uncles and close family friends are often clueless. It's a cliché but it's true: we're the last to know."

"I understand," he said, nodding now. "I'll stay alert for any signs. But Mikki's just a young woman who's changed her mind about a lot of things."

"As long as I can remember," I said, "tennis was her life. Now she's thrown it away like a crumpled candy bar wrapper."

Second frowned again. "It wasn't casual like you make it sound. She *did* love tennis. But she started to feel captive to it. And lost her interest when she started losing. I think it had a lot to do with the pressures she had on her, from her coach and even her mom and sister – when Mikki started losing, it really bummed her out. All those eyes on her, all those expectations for her – they can weigh heavily."

This kid seemed wise beyond his years.

"I will tell you one thing," he said, and his tone changed, "and it isn't any of the things you expressed concern about, Mike. Mr. Hammer. It's that damn Brian Ellis."

I cocked my head. "You're the man in her life now, Second, aren't you?"

His sigh seemed to start at his toes. "I hope I am. I seem to be. But Ellis is somebody she went steady with starting in junior high. You caught us in bed, Mike, but I'll be frank with you – Mikki has been sexually active since back then. She shared lots of years of intimacy with that creep. And they are still friendly."

I gestured to the nearby sidewalk. "Maybe not. I saw them arguing right here the other day. It got heated."

His shrug spoke volumes. "That's the kind of argument friends can have. And *exes* can have, if they haven't cut ties. You think I haven't tried to get that bum out of her life?"

"I suppose you have."

"You can *bet* I have." Another deep sigh. "But you know how it is – Ellis has a real 'bad boy' vibe that girls can't seem to resist."

Some would say that's what Velda saw in me.

"Well then, Second," I said, "you need to stay on top of your game. Edge out the competition. But to the degree that kid is still in Mikki's life, stay sharp. You see anything illegal going down – dealing, for example, on her high school campus? Or hear reliable word that her ex is peddling? You tell me. I'll come down on Ellis like a ton of bricks. And then I'll kick the shit out of him."

That made him laugh, as if I were kidding. Which of course I wasn't.

I extended my hand to him and he took it. Shook it.

"Mike… Mr. Hammer… I am glad to oblige."

We found Velda and Mikki on the couch in the living room, waiting patiently for the man-to-man between Second and me to wind up.

Her make-up perfect, at least in the slightly garish current way, Mikki – in a black/red/yellow-striped long-sleeve top and bright yellow slacks – rose and said, "If you boys have negotiated my release, can we please go? The Kingsmen go on at nine."

"Who the hell are the Kingsmen?" I asked.

"We gotta go," Mikki said, her remark getting a chuckle out of Second for some reason. Then she brushed by me, taking Second's arm and heading into the night.

Velda joined me at the door as I watched Mikki and her boyfriend walk to his Corvette. She asked, "You read Second the Riot Act?"

"Not really. Appears he already knows the facts of life." I shrugged. "He seems like a good kid."

"He's a rich one, anyway. If I ever get married, maybe it oughta be somebody rich."

"Nice to have a goal," I said, smiling, closing the door on the departing kids. "But who can put a price on my kind of charm?"

Velda and I had made it all the way through Johnny Carson on *The Tonight Show* and were in our guest-room bed, getting a good night's sleep. Or anyway I was – Velda was propped up by pillows, reading *The Love Machine* by Jacqueline Susann (I was a snoring love machine beside her).

My last thoughts before drifting off were how nice it was to be away from the big bad city and its notorious mean streets. This was a suburban world where the worst problem you had to deal with was a young woman who had decided she didn't want to play tennis anymore. Not some formerly nice girl from the Midwest who was a runaway turned hooker or a businessman pretty sure his partner was trying to have him killed.

I was deep asleep when something woke me – a kind of *thump* – out in the living room.

I sat up and grabbed my .45 from the nightstand drawer; Velda was sitting up as well, alarmed, her thick novel cast aside. The only light on was her modest bedside lamp, a tiny beacon in the guest-room darkness. The nightstand clock said it was ten after two, and that was obviously in the a.m. – nothing but darkness was edging in around the windows.

Velda slipped out of bed. She put on a diaphanous robe over her blue silk pajamas and, in her delicate feminine way, grabbed her Smith and Wesson 638 from her own bedside drawer. I was in my skivvies, in the lead, as we exited quietly into the hall. No further noises greeted us, but we'd heard something, all right.

Velda hit a switch and light flooded the living room.

"Oooooh," Mikki groaned.

The girl was on the couch – her flopping there must have been the thump that woke me and alerted Velda. Her multicolor striped long-sleeve top and blinding yellow slacks were rumpled, like she'd plucked them out of a dirty laundry basket to wear, her sandals here and there, as if she walked out of them. Her long brown hair, in a straight Cher style, was a clumpy mess. The careful make-up she'd applied before going out was gone, her pale face looking so young and yet a hundred years old.

Velda leaned next to the girl. "Darling, are you all right?"

Mikki batted the air and turned away. "Lemme alone. Lemme sleep."

Velda, those big brown eyes never looking bigger, gazed up at me, unnerved. And this woman did not unnerve easily.

"Let's get her into bed," Velda said quietly, almost a whisper.

We got her off the couch, a limp creature as if her clothes had nothing in them. We drunk-walked her to her dark room. Velda lay her on the bed, on top of the spread, and I turned on the bedside lamp. The girl reacted to it like Dracula when the sun came up, rolling onto her side, away from the light, still out but whimpering like a sick puppy.

"I'll handle this from here," Velda told me, firmly.

I knew enough not to argue with her.

I stumbled back into the guest room, turned off the two nightstand lamps, and got under the sheet and a light cover and, I'm not proud to say, went back to sleep after only a minute or two of concern for the girl delaying that. Wake me in the middle of the night, you only get so much out of me. I had learned to sleep through artillery shells landing in the Pacific, after all.

But some unspecified time later, female hands shook me awake. "Mike! Mike. Something terrible."

But the Pacific had also taught me to snap awake when the time came – you developed an inner alarm clock that started ringing when the shit went down too close to you. Still in my skivvies, I followed Velda quickly out and across the hall to the girl's room.

Velda had gotten Mikki out of her clothes and into some loose PJs and under the covers. The long hair was splayed against her pillow and she seemed to be resting, quietly and deep. At first blush it seemed like all was well, after an initial scare.

"You need to see something," Velda said, again almost a whisper, though I doubted a yell would've woken this girl.

She drew Mikki's right arm out from under the covers and slipped the big, loose sleeve up over that arm, exposing it from the bicep down, the girl not stirring a whit.

The tracks were unmistakable.

The small punctures looked pink. Those were the fresh ones. Above were scabbed-over punctures, on their way to being scars.

Through my teeth, I said, "I should shake her awake and throttle her."

"No," Velda said quietly.

The woman had a quiet firmness about her. This was her sister and most females and a lot of men would dissolve into hysterics over such a terrible discovery. But however movie-star beautiful she might be, Velda had a quiet resolve and dignity won by years of being a vice cop and then an O.S.S. agent during the war, preceding her lost years in Russia ducking the *Militsiya*.

Not to mention some harrowing shit I'd put her through.

But this was Velda's sister. Her flesh and blood. An innocent girl corrupted by scum who promised heaven and delivered hell.

Still, Vel remained calm, at least on the surface. She curled a finger at me, as if summoning a child, and I followed her into the hall. We returned to the guest room, stowed away our respective weapons, as wordless as a silent movie; then went out to sit on the same couch her sister had been sprawled upon not long ago.

"I'm going to kill somebody," I said tightly. "Some bastards are going to die."

"That's all well and good," Velda said, always the reasonable one in the partnership, "but it's not going to be Mikki."

"Of course it isn't."

"We have to help her."

"Of course we do."

Velda folded her arms, stared at nothing. "The shape she's in right now, if we wake her, shake her, it's not going to do any good. Mikki has to come all the way down from her high, which would appear to be heroin."

"Fucking smack. I'm going to kill somebody."

"You said that, Mike. Settle down."

I shrugged, spoke through my teeth. "Well, at least this explains the missing Rolex and diamond ring your mother mentioned. Mikki herself took them. Obviously."

Velda took my hand and patted it. Settled me down. "Yes, obviously. Sold them to pay off some dealer."

Somebody was going to die with a bullet in the brain, but first he was going to have a couple others someplace else, and right before the final one came he would have plenty of time to think about it. Maybe three whole seconds.

I craned my neck toward the hallway of bedrooms. "I can't just wait for morning to come, for me to confront her. Till she stumbles out. I have to do *something*. Now."

"That's what I love about you, you big lug."

She was pushing my buttons; she knew if she called me that I'd be putty in those strong, feminine hands.

"Okay," I said in surrender. "What do you want to do?"

"I'm still thinking it through, frankly. But cold turkey won't be it. Our best bet is getting her into some private rehab facility."

"Larry Snyder is the doc who straightened my drunk ass out back in '63. He's got his own clinic now. He'll help us and keep it discreet."

"Good. Good. Now *you're* thinking, too. That's our best bet." She squeezed my hand. "Look, Mike – Mikki's dead to the world right now. We couldn't wake her if we tried. Let's go back in her bedroom and be good private detectives."

"Meaning...?"

"Toss that bedroom... but quietly. Like I said, I don't think we could wake her if we wanted to. But let's see what we can turn up. A phone number, maybe. A stash of drugs we can confiscate. Who knows? But we try."

I nodded. "I'm with you, doll."

With only the nightstand lamp on, we went through everything, from the bureaus to the closet, and as Velda predicted, the slumbering girl didn't even stir.

"Let's try the bathroom," Velda said, after a fruitless half-hour search of Mikki's pink feminine bedroom. "That would afford her complete privacy."

"Good thinking," I said, and followed her there.

But the closet and the medicine cabinet gave up nothing, and I even checked to see if any meds or bath powders or any damn thing might be in a container used to store something it didn't purport to be.

"Maybe Mom's bedroom?" Velda suggested.

"Well, it's a safe enough place to hide something," I said, "with your mother in that nursing home for the time being."

Yet we found nothing there, either, though it took a good hour to go through Mrs. Sterling's things.

"What about our room?" I asked. "The guest room?"

"Unlikely," Velda said, "but we should check it."

Nothing.

And we had no better luck in the kitchen and the living room with its closet.

BABY, IT'S MURDER

We returned to the couch, Velda in her robe and me still in my skivvies, the sun threatening to come up, light starting to glow around the windows.

"Let's try her room again," I said. "If she's still sleeping the sleep of the dead, we won't likely wake her. And if we do, maybe you could paddle her ass."

"Ah, Mike," Velda said affectionately, "you are *so* old-school."

"That's right," I said, "and after graduation I got a doctorate in Tough Fucking Love."

We had another look, this time including under the bed and taking bureau and nightstand drawers all the way out to check for anything that might be secured underneath. Then I recalled an old junkie trick for hiding their stash, particularly cases like this one, where the families were respectable and the user kids were sneaky.

The window in Mikki's bedroom had horizontal blinds. I checked the valance and it came off easily. Within it I struck gold.

Or anyway shit.

Taped there in a good-sized baggie were a junkie's "works" – plastic syringe, length of surgical tubing, spoon with its bowl tip scorched beneath, Bic lighter, and three small aluminum foil packages.

"This goes in the trash," I snarled. A quiet snarl, but a snarl.

"No," Velda said softly. "Put it back. Just like you found it."

I frowned at her, not understanding.

"Please," she said. And there was a melancholy urgency about it.

"All right, doll," I said, and reassembled the valance hiding place, contents intact.

The girl was still sleeping like a baby. A baby on smack, anyway.

"Let's talk," Velda whispered, and gestured for me to follow her.

Back on the couch, the lovely brunette in the robe and me in my underwear sat and talked. Mostly I listened.

"Begin by approaching your friend Dr. Snyder," she said.

Her voice, and mine when I used it, were barely audible, as if the world out there might overhear if we weren't discreet. Or maybe that child in her heroin stupor might come back around and catch us discussing her.

"We keep this quiet," Velda said. "Keep it in the family. You can do whatever off-the-books handling of whoever's behind this you choose. I'll help you if you like, right down to burying the bodies. But let's not confront the child now. Let's play detective first. This can't have been going on for long. She doesn't have visible red scarring yet. Her track marks are white, healing pink. I'm guessing she hasn't been using for more than a couple of months. There's no dark bruising, and if she were shooting up frequently, that whole area of her arm would be look bruised, dark. She has half a dozen needle marks. I don't believe we're looking at longtime usage… not yet."

I was frowning, but it was in thought, not disapproval. "We can afford a day or two of looking into this, you think?"

"I do." Velda's sigh wasn't fun to hear. "Very short-term, though. This is fire we're playing with."

"At least we know," I said, "why she turned away from tennis, and why her grades have slipped."

"And maybe," Velda said, "why that Brian Ellis kid is still in her life."

CHAPTER SIX

Neither Velda nor I got much sleep after our discovery of the girl's "works" in that valance. And over breakfast around eight, which I cooked up for us – bacon and eggs and refrigerator biscuits – Velda and I discussed in hushed tones what our day would be, while Mikki was sleeping it off.

Sitting at the little kitchen table, Velda munched thoughtfully on a bacon strip while I proposed she keep a close eye on her sister. This was Saturday and Mikki would likely have plans with Second or maybe some girlfriends, and Velda could use her shadowing skills to keep track of wherever she might go.

"You might even spot her with her connection," I said.

"You think that's Brian Ellis, don't you?"

I buttered a biscuit. "Oh, I don't know. Maybe it's some other long-haired biker who started fucking her in junior high."

That got a little smile out of her. "You have always had such a lovely way of putting things, Mike Hammer. But I'll remind you – they are clearly estranged, those two."

I talked with my mouth full. "Doesn't mean he isn't still her connection. Hell of a way to get a girl back, hooking her on heroin."

She pointed an accusing bacon strip at me. "Why don't you suspect the *new* boyfriend? Maybe he's got a business going with a high school crowd – and college kids that funded that gold Corvette of his."

"I didn't say he was off the table as a suspect. In fact, while you're keeping eyes on Mikki, I plan to drop in on Second's old man at the family manse. Sniff around some."

Velda worked up a smirk. "Well, you may sniff Second's young stepmother, knowing the way your bloodhound's snout works. She's a former showgirl of about forty with a body by Fisher. Spends her days sunning by the mansion pool."

I raised surrender palms. "You know I'm a one-woman man, doll."

"You are now. But it took you a while."

I was in the living room with my feet up when Mikki finally emerged from the hallway looking most presentable for a little junkie who'd rolled in, in the middle of the night. I'd seen her stumble into the bathroom, spend half hour in there, then stumble back into her bedroom. Her re-emergence, looking fresh as a teenage daisy, either spoke for her recuperative powers or maybe she'd popped a little speed.

You would never fucking know that her hobby was heroin. She was beautiful, a younger Velda, just slimmer and with that long straight hair brushing her shoulders. Her lightweight baby-blue sweater was long-sleeved, of course – track marks not being in style – and her pink bell bottoms matched her pink open-toe sandals.

So fresh, so innocent.

My rage and my unhappiness dueled while I somehow managed to show neither. "Hiya, kid. Rough night?"

"Don't ask," she said with a smile, then headed into the kitchen. She returned a little later nibbling one of my biscuits. "Where's Vel?"

"Getting dressed for the day. Thought we might take in that little amusement park and see how we look in the funhouse mirrors."

A lie, of course. Oh, Velda was getting dressed, all right. But we were already on a roller-coaster ride after what we learned about this kid.

Three girlfriends picked Mikki up in their Plymouth Barracuda, a red-and-black job that shouted sex and money and irresponsible rich-ass parents. Velda was poised to go out the bungalow's back door to the garage on the alley where her Mustang awaited. Not the least conspicuous car to shadow in, but Velda knew all the tricks.

I knew a few myself.

The two-story, amber-roofed tan-brick colonial estate – which the First and Second and assorted Williamses called home – wasn't a castle exactly, but it would do till one came along. Call it a medieval fortress with air conditioning. The red-brick drive through lush grounds concluded in a circle around a central cupid fountain where shrubbery knelt in worship.

I rang the bell and the human beast that answered, apparently housebroken but just, eyed me from his battered Black boxer face with slit-eyed suspicion. His head was shaved, his jaw jutted, and his shoulders required looking at one at a time. He wore a black suit and tie, a modern variation on full butler livery. Jeeves by way of Sonny Liston. Even better was that he had learned, with patient schooling one would guess, to say, "Yes?" not "Yeah?"

"My name is Mike Hammer."

"And?"

"And I'd like to see Mr. Williams, if he's home and available. I'm his son's girlfriend's uncle."

A slight lie, but I'd told worse.

"Wait," he said, and shut the door in my face.

To his credit, he did not slam it.

Perhaps a minute later, the door opened and he said, in a rich baritone, "Mr. Williams will see you now."

Six words! That was twice as many as the total of what he'd granted me previously.

He held open the door, I stepped in, and he led the way. We were in a marble-floored entryway where an army platoon might have bivouacked. The wallpaper was a pale white with gold flocking. A crystal chandelier shimmered and a staircase wound up to heaven, or perhaps the second floor. We skirted the staircase and I was deposited in a fully outfitted gym no larger than two Vic Tannys.

The man in purple sweats on the exercise bike – going a steady if modest pace – did not pause to greet me, though greet me he did: "Mr. Hammer – this is something… of an honor…"

Not an honor – "something" of an honor. Well, a guy in my line takes what he can get.

"An honor for which of us?" I asked cheekily.

"For me… of course." He stopped and climbed off, an older version of his good-looking son right down to the close-cropped blond hair. But his grooved face made clear he'd been around a while and earned his wrinkles. Hadn't we all.

Grabbing a towel from somewhere, like Bugs Bunny in a cartoon producing a machine gun, he slung the cloth around his neck and headed over to a rowing machine. Got in, as if he had somewhere to go; but did not immediately start rowing.

"You dropped by the country club, I understand," he said, one eyebrow arched.

"I did. That's your club, I hear. And you're more than just a member."

Sitting with his hands on the oars now, he said, "I'm one of the consortium who own it. I do apologize for its rundown nature."

"Still pretty nice." I was standing arms folded, like a spotter helping him exercise. "Little long in the tooth, maybe."

He shrugged purple shoulders. "Needs an overhaul. But that's coming. The country club way of life is not going the way of the dodo, no matter what you hear. Maybe you've noticed, Mr. Hammer, but this world of ours has gone generally to shit."

He began to row. Maybe he was trying to escape the changing times. He should have tried my technique: ignore them.

"You… spoke to… my man Traynor."

"Your man?"

"Well, he works for me… at the club… can't make it very far on a… pitiful teacher's pay… good man, though."

"The ladies seem to like him."

"Any… good tennis pro… better be popular… with the… wenches."

There was a word you didn't hear much anymore: wenches.

"I was expressing my concern," I said, "for my niece. I figure as her tennis coach he might have some insights as to why she quit with such a promising future ahead of her in the sport."

What I'd learned about Mikki and the contents of that valance were nobody's business but Velda's and mine.

"She isn't… your niece, though… is she, Mr. Hammer?"

"No. Actually, my goddaughter. But my fiancée is her sister – Velda Sterling – who's staying with Mikki while their mother is hospitalized. Hip replacement surgery."

Williams climbed out of the rowing machine and walked toward the corner where a wet bar waited – doesn't every fully appointed gym have one? He gestured for me to follow, as if I were his puppy in training.

"What's your poison, Mike?" he said, back behind the counter. "May I call you 'Mike'?"

"Certainly, Garrett. Or do you prefer 'First'?"

He laughed. I'd been expecting carrot juice or some kind of tonic, but he was pouring himself some Scotch over the rocks. Johnnie Walker King George Scotch, at that.

"Pity to water it down," he admitted. "But I have my health to look after."

"Who doesn't?"

He frowned and smiled all at once. "What are you having, man? Or are you one of these wusses who won't take a drink before evening comes?"

Two stools were at the counter. I took one.

"Ginger ale and some of that Scotch," I said, "if you're feeling generous."

"Ah. A man who drinks only the finest."

"Right. Canada Dry."

My host laughed a little, taking the dig well. He was wearing Paul Newman's blue eyes on loan. Unless he'd bought the damn things.

"If you want my opinion," Williams said, "and I've shared it with Second – it's a goddamn shame that girl gave up her tennis. Saw her play many a time. The list of schools after her, big-name schools, Ivy fucking League schools, is a long one. And it isn't like she couldn't use a scholarship – Mikki doesn't exactly come from money."

"No. But she does come from good stock."

"Lovely child, absolutely." He toasted me. I toasted him back.

"But," he continued, "Second is adamant about respecting the girl's own decision in that regard. His generation doesn't view the female sex with the same narrow eyes as us older misogynist males."

"Still, he has encouraged her to stick with the sport."

"He has."

I took the bubbling glass he handed me; sipped. Said, "What do you know about this boy Brian Ellis?"

He sipped and savored and said, "White trash. Bad influence. Drinker. Pot smoker. A biker who has some kind of damn hold on the girl that Second hasn't been entirely able to break… at least as far as I know. I try to stay out of my son's way. Having a father like me, with my kind of social standing – if I might be so immodest – is no picnic."

"Easier to be First than Second."

His shrug was resigned. "I am afraid so. I really don't know what else I can tell you, Mike."

"Has your son mentioned dope peddling being a problem at Mikki's high school? I'm not talking about pot, though personally I think that's goddamn evil shit. One bad thing leading to another worse one, and worser ones."

Nodding, Williams said, "No argument. But, no – I haven't heard anything from Second that would lead me to believe Sidon High is a nest of drug-dealing vipers. And this Ellis kid is out of school, remember. It's these aging bikers running dope runs to Mexico that I hear whispers about."

"Out of high school," I corrected. "But in junior college."

"If you call that 'college.'"

I let out a breath. "Well, I won't take any more of your time, Mr. Williams."

"Garrett, Mike! Garrett. You let me know whatever you might need while you're in town. I'll put you on the dining list at the club, if you like."

"That'd be swell, Garrett."

He gestured toward the exit. "I can show you out... or summon George."

"George?"

"My butler. The colored gentleman who saw you in. He was a boxer, you know. Put Floyd Patterson on the canvas."

My head bobbed back like I'd taken a punch myself. "He beat Floyd Patterson?"

"No. Patterson beat him. But first George made him kiss that canvas."

I slipped off the stool. "I can find my own way out, if you don't mind. George sounds a little too intimidating for this light heavyweight."

Williams saluted me with his snifter of expensive Scotch. "Suit yourself. Very nice meeting you, Mike."

"Same back atcha."

When I exited the gym, George was nowhere to be found, which was what I hoped, as I had something else in mind.

She was sunning by the heated pool, its shimmer rising like heat over asphalt but more inviting. Brown as a berry, blonde as a starlet, full lips a brightly lipsticked red, this forty-something vixen in a tiger-stripe bikini had less fat on her than a filet mignon. Mrs. Garrett Williams the First had an *I Dream of Jeannie* look that gave any healthy hetero male the same wish.

Her bikini barely containing their nicely rounded contents, Tammy Williams might have been sleeping behind those Ray-Bans on that lounge chair, but she wasn't, because she said, "Well, look who's here."

The voice was husky in just the right way.

I pulled up a beach chair. "Specifically, who's here? Or generally who's here?"

She looked at me over her sunglasses. The eyes were green. Like money. "Specifically. I *am* literate, you know."

"What does that have to do with anything?"

"I read the papers. I've been reading them since I was a babe in arms."

"You're still a babe. Whose arms you're in probably varies."

She tossed off her reply. "You're Mike Hammer, all right. Not in the papers as often as when you were a young, dangerous pup… but you're him."

"I'm him," I admitted. "I'm a dangerous old dog now."

"Not so old. Not any older than me and I'm still standing."

"No, you're lounging. But don't stop. It looks good on you, Mrs. Williams."

She chuckled, pushed her Ray-Bans back in place. "Now you're just showing off. I could be a guest. I could be the help."

"Expensive help, I'd say."

She swung over to sit on the edge of the lounge. Her C-cup breasts were real; a connoisseur can tell. "Are you just here to flirt with an old married lady? Or do you have something more substantial in mind?"

"I wanted to ask you about your son."

"Second? He's not my son."

"No?"

"He's my stepson. Do you know he doesn't much care for me?"

"Well, nobody likes their wicked stepmother."

An eyebrow arched over one Ray-Ban lens. "Then why does he look at me that way?"

"What way?"

"The way you're looking at me – like you want to fuck me."

I grinned, chuckled. "First of all, I bet you get that a lot. Second of all, I don't shock that easily."

Her laugh echoed off the water. It was a nice enough laugh, but it tried a little too hard.

"Why don't I buy you a drink," she said, rising. "The pool house has a lovely bar, very well stocked."

Said my well-stacked hostess.

I looked up at her. "Your husband already plied me with drink."

"Some of that valuable Scotch, I assume. Such a show-off. I don't think it's real. These are." She pointed from one breast to the other. "Or do you need to inspect the evidence?"

"Please, Mrs. Williams. I blush easily."

Soon, I was seated on a stool across from her in the poolside cabana as she played bartender, echoing the positions her husband and I had been in not long ago. She had slipped a shortie pale-yellow terry cloth robe on; it hung open, and her breasts hung too, hovering over the counter like friendly UFOs. No surgeon had been involved with their creation – maybe God. Or the Devil. She didn't have any Scotch, so I settled for Seven and Seven.

"So then," I asked, "you and Second don't get along?"

"No, we do. About as well as possible when your mother dies under mysterious circumstances and your father marries me."

I sipped. "What mysterious circumstances were those?"

"Bad brakes. A mountain road. The perfect storm. By which I mean, there was a perfect storm the night her brakes went bad on that mountain road."

"You seem fairly unconcerned about it."

She shrugged. "They weren't my brakes." Smiled. "I make my own breaks."

You could only admire an evil bitch who didn't bother hiding either her wares or her attitude.

I asked, "Like working the Copa line and marrying a rich man? Moving into a Long Island mansion? Those kind of breaks?"

"Those kind of breaks," she admitted. Something like seriousness settled in on her attractive if hard features, her green eyes narrowing. "Look, Mike. My stepson and I aren't close. I make sure we aren't, because the last thing I need is some teenager with a hard-on crawling in bed with me."

"Understood. Your husband might notice."

She flipped a hand; her nails were the same bright red as her lipstick. "We sleep apart. Sleep issues. But we're still as conjugal as fucking hell, so don't get any ideas."

"I've had nothing but ideas since I got here."

She sipped. "I saw the articles about you and that 'secretary' of yours. I know what you've got waiting for you at home."

"Maybe I'm a hound."

"Maybe you used to be and now you're just a flirt. Listen, my husband likes it when men are attracted to me. Makes him realize how lucky he is. And you're famous. He's got a kink about that and we could probably get away with having a gay old time."

"Maybe not gay."

A pink terry-cloth shoulder shrugged. "Old expression, timeless thought. But I'm worried about Second. That girl he's going with has a nasty ex who might be capable of just about anything. And Second really is kind of... pampered."

"I'm not going to lead you astray, Mrs. Williams."

"Make it 'Tammy.'"

"Okay, Tammy. I'll tell you true – that girl you mentioned is my stepdaughter. My secretary's sister. And you already know that my secretary is more than just that."

"I see." Serious now, my new friend Tammy said, "I wouldn't

like to see Second caught in the middle here. Between this Ellis boy and your stepdaughter. And meaning no disrespect, Mike – that girl is a bad influence."

A lot of bad influence seemed to be in the air.

I asked, "What makes you say that?"

Her features took on a seriousness I didn't know they were capable of. "Don't ask me how I know this, but… I have friends who know the Ellis boy. Understand?"

I was following but pretended not to. "How so?"

The husky voice grew hushed. "Long Island isn't Manhattan. It's all spread out and it has its own social structure and all, but… look, some of the people I party with have connections that aren't social. Follow me?"

"Recreational drugs."

"You said it, not me."

"I understand you've had occasional pool parties here for Second and his high school friends."

"That's right."

"Just between us – have you seen any… recreational drugs at play at any of these?"

Firm headshake. "No. Never."

I gestured toward the pool. "You're usually around, like for the one yesterday?"

She cocked her head. "I am around, but we haven't had a pool party yet this year. Too cold, obviously."

So Mikki and Second had gone off somewhere else yesterday. I should have realized that – a girl with needle tracks doesn't go to a pool party.

Tammy was studying me now, something sly in it. Her voice dropped to a whisper, which the huskiness made play rather well. She leaned over the bar. So did her breasts.

"Uh, Mike, listen. Listen carefully. My husband may have some sexual kinks that a wife like me can play to her advantage. But he's a health nut – he's almost sixty and is staunchly against everything from pot on up. And he's drummed that view into Second."

"How can Daddy know it took with Junior?"

Both shoulders collaborated on a shrug that spoke volumes. "You can never know for sure. But there are no signs that our young man of the house is anything but a straight arrow… except maybe horny. Say, uh… was my hubby working out in his little gym?"

"Not so little. Yeah. Why?"

"He always takes a nap after a workout. Tosses a few down and goes up for a snooze. Like clockwork."

"Does he."

She touched my nose with a fingertip, then withdrew it like my skin had been hot-stove hot. "Maybe you'd like to fool around a little, Mike. Maybe I'd like to see if you can live up to your storied reputation as one of Manhattan's greatest lovers."

"I appreciate the offer, Tammy. But I'd better pass."

"It's a standing one, Mike."

I was already halfway out.

"You're telling me," I said

CHAPTER SEVEN

No excuse for it, really.

Chalk it up to me being off my home turf, or maybe letting my guard down because I'd just exited a millionaire's mansion, about to climb into the heap where I'd left it on the curving brick drive.

However you slice it, though, I was a dope. An idiot who let somebody come up from behind him and, in classic private eye fashion, sap him... sap *me*... and the only break I got was I wasn't fully unconscious when I felt the hands of two men grab me and lift me and hurl me like a sack of salt into what had to be the trunk of a car.

My car.

Before the lid slammed down, I sensed hands frisking me and the .38 Police Special on my hip holster under my sports coat got plucked off me like a metallic flower. My car keys were snatched from my already limp hand.

And now the lid came down, like a coffin sealing a guy in who wasn't quite dead yet.

We rumbled off, my two new invisible friends and me, and I

was coming fully around when I heard them up in that world beyond called the front seat, talking. Discussing my future.

My limited future.

"Do we *have* to snuff him?" a whiny male voice asked.

"Sal, we already kidnapped his ass," a deeper male voice responded irritatedly. "That makes it felony murder, you dipshit."

Sal sounded hurt, even over the throaty engine noise. "That's not nice, Lou. I deserve better, you calling me that."

"Fuck you, Sal. I'm no happier about this than you are."

We weren't going fast. This seemed to be a residential area or perhaps Sidon's diminutive downtown.

"Our bum luck," Sal said. "We hadn't been up here making a drop, we wouldn'ta been the ones close enough to catch this call."

"We're convenient," Lou said, resigned to his lot in life. "We were handy and Mr. Evello give us this job and that's all she wrote."

Sal giggled. "All *he* wrote. This Hammer wasn't all they say he is. He didn't exactly have the instincts of no cat."

"He did not," Lou said, almost cheerful now. "Surprisingly simple. Easy peezy."

"Mr. Evello" could be any one of three or four members of the Evello crime family; I'd tangled with them plenty of times and, thanks to my efforts, they weren't as powerful as they once had been. Word was they were reduced to playing middle-men for the emerging Russian mob these days. How the mighty have fallen, thought the man in the trunk of their car.

Their car or...?

My car. This was the heap. These pricks may have got the drop on me but they were sloppy. And fools to boot. Surely they'd figure Mike Hammer would have some kind of ordnance stowed in the trunk of his car.

"We better make sure," Sal said, "nobody'll be around."

"Well, we'll check, dumb-ass, won't we?"

Silence but for the easy rumble of the wheels. My souped-up buggy had a nice purr going.

Sounding hurt, Sal said, "*You're* in some friggin' mood."

"Don't hold your breath for an apology, numb-nuts. I like this as little as you. Simple drop turns into a capital crime, fuck."

Even in the trunk, Sal's sigh was audible.

"We could just make it like, you know, a warning," the whiny hood said. "Kick him, maybe stomp his gun hand till it snaps, crackles and pops, then leave him to bleed and think about it."

Rumble of wheels.

Lou said, "What I hear about Hammer is, he thinks about something like this that's gone down, he comes looking. You ever hear the story about the social club massacre? He machine-gunned a room full of goodfellas till they was good-and-dead-fellas."

"Ah, that's just a story. Never happened."

"Only 'cause nobody lived to tell the tale. You be careful when we open that trunk. Be ready. He may pop out like the worst fuckin' jack-in-the-box you ever the fuck seen."

We picked up some speed. I started to smell and hear countryside. Cramped though I was, I was in a decent place, relatively speaking. The Ford trunk was roomy and I was on my side, like a giant fetus, with my hands free. They hadn't bothered to bind me. Yes, they'd taken the .38. But the good news was that piece wasn't registered, not licensed or anything. If I'd been packing the .45, it could have been traced to me, though admittedly the barrel had been changed a number of times.

But not since I took those drug dealers out in that alley.

Was that what this was about?

Those dead dealers might have Evello ties. Maybe I'd been tracked to Velda's mom's place, and shadowed till I landed somewhere making a snatch possible without attracting attention.

This was payback, wasn't it?

The trouble was I'd been too smart for my own good. Or maybe too cheap. The .38 I kept stowed in this trunk I had shifted to that hip holster. So my firepower in this metal cage was non-existent.

We sped up for a while, a short while, then suddenly slowed.

"*This* is where we're dumpin' him?" Sal said, in stupid surprise. Not a lot of planning here, apparently, or anyway none shared with Lou's excitable assistant. "A *school?* A goddamn grade school?"

"Look at the boarded-up windows, shit-for-brains. It's closed down."

"Doesn't *look* that old."

"They opened some kind of consolidated school for Nassau County, our guy says. Closed down this and a few others. Should be nobody here. Not even a fuckin' janitor."

We slowed.

"Better not be any kids," Sal said. "I don't kill no damn kids. That's evil."

Everybody has their standards, I thought.

"There ain't gonna be no kids at a closed-down school, shithead. Jesus."

"Lou."

"What?"

"Be nice."

Long pause.

"Oh-kay," Lou said.

The car took a turn to the right and crunched over gravel.

"Why aren't you stoppin'?" Sal asked.

"Better take him around back," Lou said. "Little playground there, and nobody driving by could get even a goddamn glimpse of us. Outa sight, outa mind."

Sal sounded very nervous now. "Okay. Okay."

The heap veered off the gravel and onto slightly bumpy ground. Really slowing down. I took a couple of deep breaths. The air in the trunk was stale and stifling, but at least it was air.

The car bumped up onto what was apparently concrete and glided to a stop. Engine shut off. Lou's door opened and closed; then Sal's door, after a second, did the same. Their footsteps on paving announced them as they came around back. A key worked in the trunk's lock. Before the lid was lifted, Lou had some advice.

"I think he'll still be out," Lou said, "but don't count on it. Think about all those dead guys at that social club."

"Aw, Lou, that's just a story. It's gotta be."

The lid came up.

I came out with the tire iron in my fist, held high, like an Indian with a tomahawk in a John Wayne movie.

"Oh shit," Sal said.

He was small and skinny and pockmarked and his suit was a gray sharkskin and his tie skinny and black and the side of his head caved in like an empty cardboard box you stepped on and he was dead before he knew it. He folded up like a three-legged card table and dropped, and Lou – fat, in a herringbone sports coat and Lee slacks – turned and ran. He had a pistol in his hand, some kind of revolver, but he didn't take the time to turn and shoot.

I knelt over dead Sal, his head leaking brains, and found the revolver in his shoulder holster and removed it. I was in no hurry. Lou was fat and spooked and running for cover in a small playground of rusted metal, a slide, tire swings, a jungle gym. He had apparently decided taking cover before firing at me made more sense than standing his ground and blasting.

If he'd decided anything at all.

The revolver in my hand was a formidable one, a Colt Python, surprisingly big for a little guy like the late Sal to be packing. Maybe it was like a little-dick jerk driving a Firebird or something.

I shook myself – it'd been cramped in that damn trunk – and then went after Sal. Problem for the guy was how nothing here was anything you could hide behind – the best he could do was scramble up the ladder to the slide and position himself there, covered as best he could manage behind metal steps and curve of steel, in a position from which he could snipe down at me. A good plan, in the abstract, but when his head popped up and his pistol-in-hand pointed, I triggered Sal's ridiculously oversize Colt Python and Lou's ugly mustached puss imploded even as the head it rode exploded in a festive chunky spray like the world's most ambitious pinata.

Then the headless kidnapper, whose worries about felony murder were over, slid belly down on the slide and stopped just before the end of the thing, leaving a smeary scarlet trail like a colorful snail's slimy residue. Blood poured from his nearly headless neck at the end of the slide like an overturned can of red paint.

I left the wiped-down Colt Python near the slack fingers of the late Sal's right hand, and retrieved my .38 from where the hood had shoved it in his belt. No scenario could explain this crime scene, but that was somebody else's problem. I retrieved my key ring from where the trunk key was still in the lock and confiscated my own damn ride.

Left them there like the two dead children they were, class dismissed.

Back at the Sterling bungalow, where Velda was still away, I took a shower and got into fresh clothes. I'd brought along a second sports coat and had several polos and some black jeans. I put the things I'd worn earlier in the hamper; riding in a car trunk can create wrinkles and collect random dirt and grease, you homemakers may want to note.

I allowed myself a bottle of Miller and sat on the couch wondering if any of this would catch up with me. I was fairly keyed up but the beer settled me and I was stretched out napping there when the phone rang.

It was Pat.

"I've had an interesting report," the captain of Homicide said in a just-the-facts-ma'am manner. No English on the ball at all.

I grinned at the phone. "Have you? What's the subject? The need to re-stock the break room more frequently? The rise of juvenile delinquency in the greater Metropolitan area?"

"Go to hell, Mike," he said pleasantly. "I am, as you may recall, heading up the Narcotics task force."

"And no one could do a finer job, Captain Chambers."

"Do you happen to know a Salvatore Romano and a Louis Marino?"

"Don't believe I do."

"Well, they're bagmen and sometime dealers for the Evello Family."

"Oh, are the Evellos still around?"

"Did I already tell you to go to hell?"

"I believe you did, Pat. If I run into anybody introducing themselves as... Sal who? Lou who?"

His voice took on some edge now. "You won't be running into them except possibly at a Little Italy mortuary."

"Deceased, are they?"

"Yes, and under suspicious circumstances."

I rubbed the sleep from my eyes. "Am I supposed to know something about those circumstances?"

Pat's sigh was as long as it was familiar. "Mike, they were found dead in the playground of Sidon Elementary."

"Elementary, my dear Chambers?"

"Not funny. Not funny. It's defunct. A perfect dumping ground."

I kept my tone light. "Are you implying I dumped them there?"

"Two Manhattan Island drug dealers found dead on Long Island... while Mike Hammer is visiting. What do you have to say about it?"

"Good riddance?"

That was his fist hitting his desk. "Jesus, Mike, can't you even take a vacation without this sort of thing happening?"

"What sort of thing, Pat?"

Now his words flew: "If I were to advise the Sidon PD to pick you up and give you a paraffin test, would it show you'd used a firearm recently?"

"Probably. I was at the range a day before I came out here."

"...Okay." Another sigh. "You realize I'm not on the scene."

"Obviously."

"Maybe, with your skills as a trained detective, you might speculate on how this may have happened. Just to give law enforcement a hand. Might this be an execution of two drug dealers, for example?"

"I could take a wild stab at it for you."

"Please."

"Suppose those two picked someone up to take for a good old-fashioned ride and it didn't work out for them."

A very long pause ensued.

Then: "Mike, would you say that's what happened?"

"Could have been. Could. If I had planned an execution, I would've left a tidier scene than what you're indicating."

Another very long pause. I could damn near hear his mental wheels clanking.

"Okay, Mike," he said. "I'm not going to share certain thoughts I'm having with the Sidon authorities... unless it comes up officially. From them."

"Thanks, buddy."

"Just keep out of any further trouble while you're taking time off from work to help Velda out. Okay... buddy?"

I kept it light. "I haven't been in any trouble that I can think of, Pat, but fine. By the way, a couple of things you could help me with."

"I'm sure."

"As the grand poobah of the Narcotics task force, could you find out for me who's in back of the dealing on Long Island? I don't require facts – rumor will do fine."

"Jesus, Mike."

"Simple question."

You could almost hear his eyes glazing over.

He said, "I'll check into that."

"Promise?"

"Go to hell, Mike," he said, and was obviously about to sign off when I stopped him.

"Pat, one other thing. There's a biker who Mikki was seeing. They've broken up but he's hanging around like a bad smell. Name is Brian Ellis. He's maybe twenty, twenty-one, and enrolled at Suffolk Junior College. Run a check on him for me."

"Okay." His pencil was scratching that info down. "Why, if I might be so bold as to ask?"

"If he's dealing, he may have drawn Mikki into his net."

Alarm colored his voice now. "You're shitting me."

"No. I don't want to say any more. There are some things we, Velda and I, want to deal with ourselves. It's a family matter."

Some urgency came now: "Family matters can get out of hand, Mike. They can become police matters."

"When that's appropriate, I'll bring you in. I really will, Pat. You can trust me."

"Oh, I know there are all kinds of things I can trust you to do. That's what worries me."

But at least he said, "Goodbye," before he hung up.

BABY, IT'S MURDER

* * *

I stayed around the Sterling place all afternoon. If the local cops got wind of me on their own – Pat wouldn't clue them in, that much I knew – I wanted to make myself easily available, to deal with it head on.

Nobody showed. No squad car pulled up. And the phone never rang. Home free? I could only wonder.

Around four that afternoon, Velda came in, looking troubled and, for her, less than fresh. In one of those white silk blouse and black skirt combos she often wore to work, she might have stepped out of the office. She joined me on the couch. Sat close and rested a hand on my arm.

"Well," she said, going straight to it, "Mikki did go to the mall all right, and she and her girlfriends did the typical high school stuff – trying things on, shopping, sitting at a table in the mall court sipping Cokes and giggling. Couldn't have been more wholesome – a bunch of Bettys and Veronicas."

"But?"

"But." The dark almond eyes bored into me. "The girlfriends left without her and she met with the Ellis boy in the back mall parking lot."

I couldn't hold back the sneer. "Ellis 'boy.' He's of age – a college student. Go on."

Her head tilted toward me, the arcs of raven hair framing the lovely, troubled face. "I parked – it was fairly busy back there, and I made sure I wasn't seen, kept well enough away to watch but not close enough to hear. They were standing talking near the double doors into Bloomingdale's, under an overhang. The angle was such that I couldn't lip-read."

Like a lot of investigators, Velda's lip-reading skills were formidable.

"They seemed to be arguing," she went on, eyes tensed in thought now. "I may be assuming too much, but from gestures Mikki made to her purse, she seemed to be broke, and perhaps begging for him to supply her on credit. Just a guess, Mike."

"An educated one."

She let some air out. "At any rate, I didn't see him hand her anything. If Mikki's broke, she didn't talk him into a one-way deal, at least that I saw. I suppose he could be trying to leverage her out of that relationship with Second, so our biker friend could get back in the game."

I frowned. "If they were an item, would Ellis supply her in exchange for sex, you think?"

Velda opened her hands. "Who can say? I don't think she's a hardcore addict, not yet – the tracks on her arm don't indicate that, anyway. But you know, Mike, and I know – junkies will do *anything* for a fix."

No question about it. If you took drugs out of the equation, the World's Oldest Profession would be doing considerably less business.

"And if that jerk loves her," I said, "what some guys will do for love isn't written in any rule book."

"No." She shook her head and the black scythe blades of her hair swung. "I feel like we're on the verge of something happening, something… not good." Her dark-eyed gaze fixed itself on me.

"Can you make a phone call to your friend, Dr. Snyder? We've got to get that girl into rehab before she gets in any deeper."

"I'll make the call," I said, got up, and headed for the phone.

Velda was on the edge of the couch. "Do you think he can help her?"

"Doll, if he can dry a dipso like me out, he can do just about anything."

I made the call.

CHAPTER EIGHT

When Mikki came home later that afternoon, we were ready, or as ready as anybody could be. Velda had said to me, "Let me handle this," and I'd agreed to that. Promised not to go ballistic even if I felt like the countdown had started.

Then the girl came smiling in the door, looking fresh and innocent and as wholesome as Sandra Dee, all baby-blue sweater (long-sleeved), pink bellbottoms and open-toed sandals. Her eyes were dark and bright, her long black hair brushing her shoulders, her lips a frosty pink. There she was, Miss Teen America.

I was standing at one end of the couch and Velda the other and in front of us was a low-slung coffee table...

...with the baggie of the girl's "works" – syringe and tubing and scorched spoon and Bic lighter and aluminum packets of H – set out there like the accusation they were.

Her smile froze as her eyes took in the junkie's kit and then dissolved into something slack yet filled with fear and dismay and a thousand other emotions.

Velda gestured to the couch. "Have a seat."

Mikki didn't move for ten long seconds, then shut the door, but just stood there as she said, "I can explain."

I said, "You heard your sister. Sit down."

Velda gave me a little take-it-easy look but it was hard for me. I was boiling.

The teenager came over and sat in the middle of the couch and Velda sat next to her on one side and I did so on the other. Velda's hands, almost prayer-like, were in her lap. My hands were in my lap, too. Fists.

"Just listen," Mikki said, her voice soft, serious. "A girl friend of mine at school... I don't want to say her name, I think you'll understand... I'm keeping those things for her. That's the start and finish of it."

Velda said nothing.

I said nothing.

"Look," Mikki said, and her gaze swung from Velda to me and back again, "she's really a nice girl and she's trying to quit using that stuff and that's why it's with me and not her. I know it sounds crazy, but that's the truth, really, it's the truth. *I* would never do that kind of thing. You can't *believe* that about me."

Velda pulled back the right-hand sleeve of her sister's sweater and revealed the tracks, the bruising, the red spots. The girl gasped at the sight, as if seeing those telltale marks were a surprise to her.

Then the child hung her head. Her hands were on her thighs, trembling. Her voice was small. "All right. It's mine. It's mine. That stuff is all mine." Then she raised her head and leaned toward Velda. "But I'm not an addict! I'm *not!*"

"We're not going to judge you, honey," Velda said, taking one of the girl's hands.

I was ready to judge the little brat. I was ready to put her over my knee and blister her ass! But this was Velda's show, not mine.

"I was depressed," Mikki said in an apologetic, Principal's Office way. "My grades were bad, probably because I was spending all my time on my tennis. Eating nervously. And then I started losing games... I'd gotten so, so, so very *fat*... I tried some pills and they didn't work and then somebody, do not ask me who, suggested China white. He said it was like heroin but safer, and I could just use it sparingly, to help me lose weight and give me a boost when I needed it. And I'm not hooked, Vel! Mike, I'm really not!"

"You have to quit," Velda said.

She nodded and nodded some more. "I know. I will. I'll quit right now!"

I said, "Who is the somebody who suggested China white? What's his name?"

The girl's tortured expression begged me. "Mike, I can't tell you. I don't want to get anyone else in trouble. I'm... I'm sure he was just trying to help."

"Damnit – you need to tell me."

"No, Mike. I can't!"

On the other side of her, Velda was giving me a look and shaking her head. I backed off. But I was trembling as bad as the girl was.

"I'll stop right now," Mikki said. "We'll flush that stuff and the rest down the toilet! Okay? Are we good?"

"Not that easy," I said.

Velda said, "We've lined up a place for you to get better. A kind of hospital."

She shook her head, all that long black hair shimmering. "No. No. Rehab? I don't need it. I'm not that bad. Just an occasional user. Not some kind of... of addict or anything."

"You're going," I said.

"No! No..."

Velda put her arm around the girl, saying, "It'll be all right, honey."

Finally came the tears – a torrent of them accompanied by racking sobs. She waved loose, dismissive fingers at the "works" on the coffee table. "I don't need that! I don't want that! I'm not some kind of low-life junkie or anything. I'll stop, I'll stop! You have to believe me, I'll *stop*!"

I said, "You wouldn't like cold turkey."

That alarmed the girl. "What?"

Velda gave me another look. "Sweetie, you won't have to go cold turkey. You're not looking at terrible withdrawal pains. This is a kind of hospital. They'll ease you off. They'll help you. They'll get you back in shape again. You'll be back on the tennis court before you know it."

Mikki's eyes and nostrils flared. "I don't want to play fucking tennis! You're terrible! You're *both* terrible! I thought you loved me, Vel! But all I am is an *embarrassment* to you."

"Honey, we do love you," Velda said. "We're going to get you help."

Mikki's lower lip, the pink gloss gone, was trembling. "Well... if... if that's what you think is best..."

Through my teeth, I said, "Who gave you the China white?"

She screamed. It was like something out of a horror movie. Truth is, it scared me a little.

Velda frowned in my direction and said, "Never mind that. Mike's just a little upset about the idea of anybody leading you astray."

Astray? Somebody had turned this sweet kid into a junkie, and by God, whoever he was, I'd give him the kind of quick death that was merciful considering the slow death he'd been peddling.

Velda asked, "You cool, Mike?"

"As a cucumber," I said.

Mikki was settling down, drying her eyes with a tissue, when Velda said to me, "I'm going to help Mikki pack some things. Then we'll drive her out to your friend's clinic."

"It's a plan," I said.

Velda helped her sister out of the living room and into the hall and the girl's room while I sat there clenching and unclenching my fists.

They had been in there maybe five minutes when I heard the screech of wheels outside, sounding so close to the house a vehicle might have crashed through the front door. I ran to our guest room and grabbed my .45 from the nightstand and ran into Velda in the hall.

"What is it?" she asked, eyes wide.

The gun was in hand, pointing up. "Not sure. Stay with the kid. She might go out a window or something."

Velda nodded and went back into Mikki's bedroom while I headed outside.

Second's gold Corvette was the apparent source of the screeching wheels. It was angled up over the curb and onto the sidewalk and into the yard somewhat, easily trumping the time that Ellis kid had parked his bike on the lawn.

The rider's side door seemed to fling itself open and Second stumbled out. I went to him quickly and prevented him from taking a header onto the sidewalk.

He was a mess.

A bloody mess, his floral shirt and white jeans rumpled, torn, dirt-smudged, scarlet-splotched. He wore only one shoe, the remainder of a pair of expensive running trainers, his other foot bare. His eyes were swollen almost shut, the right eye blackened, his nose trailed red, his lips puffy.

Somebody had beaten the ever-loving shit out of him.

I shoved the .45 in my waistband and slipped my arm around his shoulder and steadied him. "Let's get you inside, kid."

He didn't argue.

I drunk-walked him up the front walk and the short flight of stairs and over the stoop into the bungalow – I'd left the door open. Helped him in, gesturing to the couch where Velda and I had sat with Mikki.

"No," he said, and he raised a hand with skinned, puffy knuckles in protest. "I'm... I'm on my way to the emergency room."

"That's a good idea. I'll drive you."

"No, no need. Just give me a minute. I... I wanted to warn Mikki." He looked toward the couch where the junkie stash on the coffee table made a profane centerpiece. "You... you *know* about Mikki, then."

"I do. Sounds like you did, too, Second."

The boy was trying to look at me, but lifting his head up enough was a chore. "I... I've been trying to... trying to get her to quit. But she wouldn't hear of it. Mikki's hooked but doesn't think she is."

"I think she may be getting the picture now."

"Really?" His eyes came alive in their puffy settings. "That would be great. That would be fantastic."

"Why did you head here, Second? Somebody obviously gave you a hell of a beating."

"I... I wanted her to go to the cops about her old boyfriend."

I frowned. "Ellis. Brian Ellis is her connection?"

Second nodded.

Not a surprise.

"Him and some of his biker buddies waylaid me and did this to me. Half a dozen of them. I fought back, for what good it did me. I wanted to warn Mikki she might be in danger from him. He might've heard her talking about trying to kick the stuff."

"You think he'd give her a similar makeover?"

His eyes popped in the puffing. "I think he might *kill* her! If he thought she might rat him out to the cops, he would, no question! He's got half a dozen kids at the high school dealing for him – he was the biggest pusher around when he was going there. Somebody's got to stop that bastard!"

"Where can I find him?"

"There's a biker bar in downtown Sidon. That's where I tracked him down, and that's where Ellis and his buddies beat the crap out of me in the alley behind. Fucking cowards, four of them to one lousy me."

"These the biker crowd he hangs with?"

"Well, they're dealers under him. At biker bars and near high school and college campuses. They don't wear their leathers and such peddling at those last two venues."

Velda came out from Mikki's room. "Is everything okay?" she asked from the mouth of the hallway. "Second! Are you all right?"

"He's on his way to the emergency room," I told her. "Go back and ride herd on Mikki. I don't want her seeing him."

Velda nodded and did that. She'd been in charge where Mikki was concerned; but she knew this thing had taken a turn into my territory.

With a row of Harleys along the building's side wall, Wallace McBeery's looked to have been part of the Sidon downtown strip long enough for its name to have once resonated. That exterior wall of the corner joint was gray-painted brick, the front darker gray clapboard. A sign advertised LIVE MUSIC but wasn't specific, and the single, rather small window said HAMM'S and suggested things might be happening inside that shouldn't be seen from the outside.

I went in anyway.

The joint, no darker than your average closet, had a narrow layout, as if it had once been two lanes of a former bowling alley, with a barely raised stage at the far end. The floor was part pine, part cigarette ash, all broken dreams. You could get a blow job here or get rolled or maybe shot and nobody would mind, long as you kept it to yourself. Moving past the ancient wooden bar, you could make out the razor blade lines indicating more than one kind of Coke got served up here for those not interested in the warm beer or watered liquor.

The bartender was the only female in the place at this slow moment, a gal of thirty who looked forty with red hair permed sometime this century and a nicely filled black bra under a denim vest, sleeveless, to better show off the Tweety Bird tattoo on her left arm and Sylvester the Cat tattoo on her right arm. I stopped and bought a bottle of Miller from her; her smile was as yellow as Tweety but the rest of her would do in a pinch. Christmas lights, ample wood paneling and a few bar games completed the picture.

On a weeknight, around six in the off-season, the place wasn't doing much business. Half a dozen bikers in well-worn leather jackets and denim jeans and boots were leaning against the bar, which had no seats and made them look like they meant business. That business, I figured, was almost certainly selling smack and other nasty goodies. It occurred to me I could unload my .45 on all six of them and the future of Western Civilization would not suffer for it; maybe improve.

I was in a mood.

The booths past the bar hugged the walls to make room for an excuse for a dance floor, though I had a hunch that area mostly showcased fights. Well, one man's entertainment is another man's autopsy report. Those booths would sit two comfortably and four if you weren't picky about who you rubbed against. Brian Ellis was in one, nursing a bottle of Pabst.

That he'd been in a fight was apparent, but that he'd given better than he'd got also seemed evident – some bruising here, a contusion there, on his boyish, slightly bearded face. That was about it. His hair was out of the ponytail and hanging straight now, giving him an Indian vibe. His leather vest and long-sleeve t-shirt and denims did have a rumpled look, but nothing like Second's.

"Don't say I oughta see the other guy," I said, sliding in, having to speak up over heavy metal rock playing on a jukebox. "I already have. And you and your buddies gave him a hell of a beating."

Whole lotta love, the jukebox screamed.

Ellis cocked his head, narrowed his eyes. "What buddies, Mr. Hammer?"

Was he shitting me?

I said, "This is a funny fucking place to be calling somebody 'Mister.'"

"You have the wrong idea about me, Mr. Hammer. You really do." He shrugged; he seemed depressed. His right hand held onto the bottle of Pabst; his long-ago injured limp left arm hung.

"Maybe," I said, "I got the wrong impression seeing the kind of place you frequent."

He gestured with the hand he still had. "They treat me like a human being here. And it's the only place in Sidon where a guy like me can get served."

"What kind of guy is that?" I asked. "It's not like you're under-age."

"Just what you see, Mr. Hammer. A long-haired fucking freak. A would-be outlaw biker."

Born to be wild, the jukebox said.

I looked at him carefully. Something was off here. My brain started working.

"What happened," I said, pressing him, "between you and Second?"

"What do you think? I kicked his ass."

"Not easy with one hand and without six buddies."

He shrugged. "Nobody helped me. I have a good right. And two steel-tipped toes. Also, Second's a wuss."

That actually got a smile out of me. "Any special reason why you kicked his ass?"

The boyish face frowned into something older. "What do you think, Mr. Hammer? Because of what he's done to Mikki."

I leaned forward. "*What* has he done, Brian?"

He snorted a laugh; chugged some beer. "Like you'd believe me."

"Try me, kid. If you think I never rode a Harley, you'd be wrong. Hell, I used to race stock cars."

His eyebrows raised in skepticism. "*You* raced stock cars?"

"Till I crashed one and almost bought the farm."

He laughed, not that there was much humor in it. "You don't seem like a Hell's Angel type, Mr. Hammer."

"I'm not. Like I said, stock cars were my passion, till one almost killed me. But I was a motorcycle cop once upon a time. Before I got assigned to a desk for being too big a hard-ass."

Ellis was looking at me the way a dog tries to understand its master. "Are you saying you don't assume I'm the bad guy in this?"

I smirked and there was little humor in that, too. "Maybe I did until… I don't know. I've been in the P.I. game a long time and I learned early on not to take things at face value."

That amused him, but bitterly. "You mean, like a nice kid like Mikki Sterling can sometimes be a hype. Notice I say 'hype,' not 'doper,' 'cause she's moved way past grass and a few diet pills."

Bad moon rising...

"You were seen arguing with her, Brian, more than once. You're saying you were trying to stop her using? To stop her... from what? Seeing Second?"

His nod came slow. But sure.

"Goddamnit, *he's* the dealer," I said, and slammed my fist on the booth top, making our bottles of beer jump. "Somebody told me once not to judge a book by its cover."

Someone wise named Velda.

Ellis shook his head, once. "Second's not a dealer, exactly. He's the supplier, but more than that. He's the boss of a... a network of young-looking guys who pose as high school students."

I frowned, trying to process that. "Young enough to hang around school yards, you mean? And not get noticed?"

The young man waved that off. "Oh hell, no. Second gets them enrolled under fake names with detailed documentation. Phony transcripts, background info, the works."

I was still having to talk above the jukebox. "If you knew all this, why didn't you go to the authorities? Or, hell – come to *me*, once I got to Sidon?"

Now he was emphatically shaking his head. "Mr. Hammer, how am I to know what authorities to trust? This is a widespread enough deal that some cops on the take just *must* be involved. And as for going to *you* about it – no offense, but you didn't come off as being real open-minded or anything."

...evil ways...

"I guess I didn't," I admitted, not proud of myself. "Listen, son – I have contacts in law enforcement, reliable ones I can guarantee aren't bent. I can work this from my end and get Second and his entire network of dealers exposed."

Now he was leaning forward. "What can I do to help, Mr. Hammer?"

I raised a lecturing forefinger. "You can lie low till you hear from me. Write down your phone number and address on a napkin and I'll be in touch."

He did that, and asked, "I guess I lost my temper, beating Second up like that. It was all I could think of to do. Sorry."

"Nothing to apologize for," I said. "I'd have killed him. I still may."

CHAPTER NINE

Lights were winking on like fireflies in the quiet suburban Sunrise Hills neighborhood at dusk as I pulled the heap in behind Velda's Mustang at the Sterling bungalow. All seemed right in this quiet world.

Then why wasn't Velda on her way to Dr. Larry Snyder's clinic with Mikki by now? There hadn't been enough time to make that trip and back again. Just getting the girl admitted would make that unlikely.

An uneasiness quickened my step up the sidewalk and the short flight of steps onto the porch, and I had moved my .38 from the hip holster to my hand before I went in, low and ready.

On the living room floor, amid the little-old-lady curios and plastic-covered furnishings, was the garish cover of a true-crime magazine come to life.

Velda lay just this side of the couch – her whole body, head first, belly down, pointed toward the mouth of the hallway connecting the bedrooms. The white silk blouse bearing a few telltale blood droplets, black skirt hiked and exposing lovely legs, she lay sprawled like a runner caught in motion – not that she was going anywhere. Her kitten heels were off and askew and a blade of raven hair somewhat obscured her face. Above her left ear, like a ghastly flower in her hair, was a ragged red circle, matted but for an oozing center.

I knelt over Velda and said her name, first a cry of anguish from deep within me, then various levels of volume as if that mattered, as if a whisper were better than a scream.

Reluctant to move her, I holstered the .38 and lifted her nonetheless and lay the woman out on the same couch where we'd confronted Mikki not long ago. The girl's junkie "works" were still there like an obscene centerpiece. I slipped a throw cushion under Velda's head to keep it slightly elevated, her face toward me as if she were blissfully asleep, a condition belied by the blossom of scarlet in her hair.

Weapon back in hand, I quickly but carefully checked the rooms. Nobody was present, nothing else seemed amiss, with one exception. In Mikki's bedroom, the girl's suitcase lay open on the bed like a yawning mouth, partially filled with clothes while some other things were stacked alongside waiting to be packed. Clearly the girl had been interrupted.

So had Velda.

I went to the phone in the kitchen and dialed 9-1-1.

The heap rode the rear of the screaming ambulance all the way to the Sidon Medical Center; then I was sitting in the waiting room among other worried souls. Half an hour or so went endlessly by before a middle-aged female doctor in whites approached, stethoscope around her neck, clipboard in hand.

I stood.

BABY, IT'S MURDER

The doctor looked at me with clear blue eyes that had seen too much in their day, and her short gray-streaked black hair stood up like she'd been frightened once and it stuck. There was something *Bride of Frankenstein* about it.

But the woman's voice was businesslike with a cushion of compassion—exactly right, not that it helped. "You're Mr. Hammer?"

"Yes. How is she?"

"You checked her in?"

"Yes. How is she?"

"Not next of kin?"

"No. Fiancée. *How is she?*"

She decided to tell me. "Miss Sterling appears to have a concussion and will need to stay with us overnight for observation. Needed a few stitches, but all in all, the prognosis is good."

"That's a relief to hear. But is she conscious?"

A cautious nod. "Yes, in and out. We've sedated her, mildly – anything too extreme in that regard might mask symptoms."

"Could I sit with her?"

The doctor indicated the direction from which she'd come. "We haven't moved Ms. Sterling to a private room as yet. Right now she's here in our triage ward. It's snug but you're welcome to stay with her. Understand, you may be asked to leave at any moment."

I nodded.

The doctor had a nurse escort me to Velda's curtained cubicle among half a dozen others. As promised, it wasn't roomy, but the closer I could be to her, the better. She was on her side, the shaved place evident where a bandage had been applied to the stitched wound. A single chair was available and I pulled it close, sat and held her hand. When those big brown eyes snapped wide open, I almost jumped.

"*Mike…*"

"Take it easy, baby. You're in good hands. Mine included. This is the Sidon hospital. You up to telling me what happened?"

She started looking around, though the effort made her wince. "Mikki – where's Mikki?"

"Not here. And she wasn't with you. You were alone in the house. I found her suitcase, half-packed."

Her mouth pursed, as if she tasted something very sour.

"Second," she said, bitterly, collecting thoughts that were surely scattered. "Mike, he's not what we thought he was."

"No. I confirmed that with the Ellis boy."

"You believe the Ellis boy?"

"I do. He told a convincing tale and I buy it all the way – Second is not only Mikki's connection, he's got his dirty little fingers in the drug traffic at high schools and colleges all over Long Island. He's a mini-fucking-kingpin. We'll get him. Don't worry. We'll stop him. He's who sapped you?"

Her nod was small but it spoke volumes. "Mike, Mikki wasn't complicit. You need to know that! Second was dragging her out of her bedroom into the hall when I tried to stop him and instead he stopped me. Hit me with… something."

She raised a hand toward the bandaged wound but didn't touch it.

"I got played for a sucker," I said. Then I shook my head. "No. I played *myself* for a sucker. I looked at long hair and motorcycle boots and saw a creep. I took a clean-cut kid at face value and bought in whole hog. Forgot every suspicious instinct that's fared me so well over the years."

"Mike... Second hit me with something..."

"You said that."

Was she getting ready to pass out again?

"No," Velda said firmly. "You aren't following. He hit me with... it must have been *your* .45. Slapped me with it. The barrel of it..."

She closed her eyes.

When were they going to have a room ready for her, anyway? The sounds and smells of this triage area were unnerving. Alarms and beeps, low tones, high-pitched ones, dissonant and shrill and constant. Noise from patients, noise from staff. Antiseptic smells, with a biting edge, the artificial fragrances of soaps and cleaners hiding fecal sins... tired... so tired...

"Mike... Mike..."

I sat up. I was still seated next to Velda, but we were in an actual hospital room now. A private one. She was hooked up to the usual machines, and propped up a little with a pillow, keeping her head higher than the rest of her, as I'd done. The sounds of those machines were muted, the air cool.

"How did I get here?" I asked, scratching my head.

Velda smiled, an angel in a white hospital gown. An angel with a bandaged head. "Shouldn't I be the one asking that?"

"Tell me they didn't wheelchair me in here. I got a reputation to protect."

Her smile wrinkled one side of that lovely face. "No, I believe you came under your own steam. Half asleep, though."

I sat up. My mouth tasted like I'd been sucking on an inner

tube. I began to rise. "I should let you get some rest."

"Don't go just yet."

"I, uh… have things to do."

Places to go, people to kill.

"Please, Mike. Stay."

"Sure, doll." I settled back; my chair had just the right amount of padding for hospital-room seating – enough to be temporarily comfortable without encouraging visitors to stay long.

"I'm going to be fine now," Velda said.

And her voice sounded surprisingly strong.

"But *you* have to go," she said, almost scolding.

Wasn't that what I'd started to do before she stopped me? Had that blow to her head made her loopy?

"You have to go and find Mikki," Velda said. Orders from headquarters. "Bring her back. Bring her back to me, Mike."

I was sitting forward again. "Of course I will. You know I will. Whatever it takes."

"But not just yet…" She was looking past me. "I've been thinking, Mike. Thinking ever since I got to Sidon. I believe… I believe it's time."

"For what, doll?"

Now her gaze returned to me. Something unsettling about it…

"Time to own up," she said. "Time for a little… truth telling."

I grinned at her uneasily. "What are they pumping into you through that IV, anyway?"

A small smile came and went. "No, I've been mulling this ever since I got back to Mom's this trip."

I stood, leaned a hand against her bed.

BABY, IT'S MURDER

"Listen, baby, you better take it nice and easy, like Sinatra says. You need your rest. Just get some sleep and let these medics take care of you. You can bet I'll get your sister back, safe and fucking sound, and that damn kid Second and whoever else is behind this is going down for the long drop."

But it was almost like she wasn't listening. Wasn't like she hadn't heard me spout off like that before.

"Mike... about my sister..."

"I told you. I'll find her and those that took her will—"

"Yes." She was smiling, but it was just barely a smile. Rather a Mona Lisa kind of unknowable thing. "About Mikki... there's something I need to tell you. Something you need to know."

What the hell was this? Maybe she got sapped harder than the docs realized.

"What do I need to know, doll?"

She gestured. "Better take a seat, Mike."

Something about the tone, both distant and in my face, set my ass back down in that chair. Like right now.

Her voice was so hushed it claimed my attention, like a priest in a confessional: "Just listen. Please listen. And don't judge. I know you, Mike Hammer, and you're the jury and all that goes with it. But for once... don't judge. Don't judge *me*."

I was shaking my head. "I would never do that, kitten."

An eyebrow arched. "You *might*... so listen. Just listen." Her voice was soft and barely audible, and yet in a way she projected it at the top of her lungs, rattling the cages of my existence. The story she told... well.

Judge for yourself.

"Years ago... almost two decades ago," Velda said, "I had to go west to help my aunt. My sick aunt, remember? No, don't answer. I know being without me for those months was hard on you. But you were, at least for you, understanding. Supportive. I'd always been close to my aunt and I told you she was very sick and she needed me. You offered to hire a nurse but I insisted on doing it myself... like now, when I wanted to come home and help Mom out after her hip surgery, and look after Mikki... you understood. Tough for an only child like you, but you did. You did. Thing is, Mike – it was just a story. My aunt wasn't sick at all. I was the sick one. Well. Not sick exactly... pregnant."

It was a gut punch. I was shaking. Not with anger or rage or even surprise for that matter. Just shaking.

"Mom went with me, remember?"

I nodded, numbly.

"Mom came home with the late-in-life baby she'd had. Hadn't realized it when she went out west with me, to help out my aunt. No idea that she was pregnant, she told the world. My daddy didn't know, either, but he was thrilled. That was the story. But it was a lie."

I was shaking. I was goddamn shaking.

"*I* had a baby, Mike – our baby, yours and mine. I named her 'Mikki' after her grandfather who everybody called Mickey. You can figure out the rest. I brought the little girl home and she was a sister to me and my mother was a mother to her, and my police officer daddy went along with it. He died on the job, heroically, not long after. You stepped in to a degree. You were... you were her godfather, her 'unofficial uncle,' and someone Mikki and I could always depend on. Who the girl could look up to, this famous, notorious, adventurous man. Do you understand, Mike?"

How can you be furious with a woman who's lying in a hospital bed? With her sweet head bandaged? How could I ever be furious with this woman at all? But I was astounded and hurt. Most shit rolls off of me, but this... cut deep. Wounded me. Rocked me.

I sat back in my barely padded chair. Not anger. No anger. Disappointment. Shocked realization.

My voice never trembles. But it did then.

"Why, Velda? Why would you do that? I would've embraced that little girl. She would have been *ours*. We would have raised her together. How could you... *deny* me that? Deny *us* that?"

I could barely see her through something in my eyes.

"Because, Mike," Velda said, and she was as stern and loving as a stern, loving parent, "eighteen years ago you were a psychotic and a drunk. A recovering drunk... but an acute alcoholic fighting the urge every day."

She wasn't wrong.

"You were a man taking on the world, cleansing it of the 'evil ones' whenever they made the unwise decision to get in your line of fire. You were a man laughing in the face of death. And I thought, I *really* thought, I would lose you someday to that madness. But I didn't. At least not yet I haven't. And I am so glad. Or maybe... relieved? I could never resist you, Mike. And perhaps I suffered from a milder case of that same madness. So how could I expose my daughter to that kind of danger?"

"Our daughter," I corrected, sullenly.

For a moment bitterness touched her expression. "You don't even remember the night we conceived our daughter, Mike – you didn't even remember being with me that one time, at all. Do you recall that night even now? That terrible, lonely night, when so many men died, and you rescued me, my knight in… shabby armor. That was the first time, the only time in those days, that you threw any hesitation between us out the window…" Then archness colored her tone. "…and the fair maiden willingly rewarded Saint George, didn't she? And the next morning? Nothing from you. Like the blackout drunk you could still be back then. And this was tomorrow and I was still your holy virgin. The pistol-packing Madonna you whored around on." She raised her hands, palms out, as if in surrender. "No, no, no judgment. Not from me, so none from you, if you don't mind. I loved you then and I love you now. I knew you were a lot of things, Michael Hammer – hero, villain, and so much in between… just not a father. Not then."

This time my whisper shouted.

"I'm ready now," I said.

The almond eyes narrowed, this beauty with the bandaged head. "Maybe. But look at the life we lead. Look at where we are right now."

"It's the path we chose."

"Yes it is," Velda said, and nodded as much as she dared. "And there was never any room for a family on it."

A machine beeped its ellipsis.

I stood. "I'll find her, kitten. I'll get her back. Then we can sort this out. Right now, Second or somebody he works with is holding her. Maybe the plan is for Mikki to turn up an overdose victim, a fatality of her own frailty. Maybe she's been booked on a tramp steamer to some overseas hellhole to sell herself at some pimp's pleasure. Whatever sick shit Second's got in mind, I swear to you I will stop it. You think I was a psychotic in the old days, doll, get ready for the sequel."

I rose and started for the door.

Velda called out to me. "Mikki went under duress, Mike. Remember that! This is not a young woman under that nasty brat Second's spell. She'll cooperate with whatever you need to get her out of there, wherever 'there' is."

I turned and looked back at her. "I know. Look, Velda, you're safe here. If they release you before I get back, go home and stay put till you either hear from me or, maybe, Mikki."

Her eyes flared with hope. "You think I might? Might hear from Mikki?"

"I do."

Velda, bandaged or not, sat up sharply. "Mike… you think it's possible Mikki could find some way to escape on her own?"

I was halfway out when I said it: "She's our daughter, isn't she?"

CHAPTER TEN

I returned to the bungalow almost by rote. I didn't know where else to start. Around me, that quiet suburban world seemed already asleep with only a few lights on and just the muffled sounds of a TV across the way to break the night noise. I slid the heap in behind Velda's Mustang as before, and headed inside. Entering into the living room, all looked normal, the expected little-old-lady habitat. But on the carpet to the right of the couch, where Velda had laid, were little brown-red spots, blood spatter from where my .45 had clouted her courtesy of that clean-cut college boy I'd trusted, Garrett Andrew Williams the Second.

Or *had* it been my .45?

Velda only glimpsed the weapon. So I checked the guest room where she and I had been camped out, went directly to the night stand where I'd been keeping the .45... and it was, indeed, gone.

The .45 that phony prick wielded had been mine, all right.

Did Second take it to keep me from it? Had he come back to the bungalow after I left, slipped inside while Velda and Mikki were busy packing, and taken a look around the guest room? And confiscated my .45 for his own purposes?

If he'd had no gun of his own with which to face Velda down, that made sense. Sort of. Could there be any other reason why he'd want my .45, that fabled weapon the New York tabloids had once made such a fuss about? Had Robin Hood's bow and arrow found itself in the Sheriff of Nottingham's hands?

I couldn't make heads nor tails of it.

While I was in the guest room, I took the opportunity to get the box of .38 cartridges I'd stowed in my suitcase, a precaution reflective of that constant paranoia someone like me carries with him along with his firearms and bad attitude.

But I'd also brought along a box of .45 cartridges – smaller than a pack of cigarettes, with the familiar MATCH and eagle as the front logo and the side designation:

50 CARTRIDGES
BALL M 1911
BULLET 230 GRAINS
VELOCITY 820

But the box was empty.

And it had been shy only of the eight rounds I'd kept loaded into my missing .45.

The similar box of .38 cartridges, however, was missing only the six rounds in my hip-holstered Police Special revolver. I stuffed the little box in my left-hand pants pocket.

My gun hadn't been all Second wanted – he gathered the ammo, too. I could picture him dumping the box of bullets into his palm like pills from a medicine bottle, then shoving them into a pocket.

Maybe to further disarm me? He might not know I'd been carrying a .38, despite the other ammo box.

But he should have. I may have been on a sort of vacation or sabbatical, but my adversaries might still be on the job, as this situation proved. So I'd be packing something.

Such is my paranoid thinking... and it's served me well.

Though I'd given the place a cursory once-over before getting help for Velda and following that help to the hospital, I figured I better give Mikki's bedroom an in-depth look. Maybe, thin as the possibility might be, there might be some small clue to indicate where she'd been taken. In my experience, I'd seen a matchbook lead to the electric chair and a notepad slip to a life sentence.

But before I could look at Mikki's living space from a detective's point of view, it suddenly hit me in an entirely different way.

From a father's point of view.

This was a teenage girl's bedroom with its pink walls and Beatles poster and blue nubby bedspread and the stand with portable record player perched. The fragrance of a young female wafted like pleasant smoke, soap and perfume and powder and clean sheets and I sat on the edge of her bed and maybe I wept for a while. You can't prove I did. But maybe.

Then I got mad, mad at Velda for not sharing her secret sooner, almost two decades sooner, and I was pounding a fist on the bed and its mattress squeaked, taunting me, and finally any anger I felt about what Velda had denied me, had denied us, dissipated.

She had been right, after all.

When she came home to me after disappearing into that pit the Soviets call Russia, she'd found a drunk, a husk of what had been me, skinny, crazy... but hadn't I been crazy before? After the war, I'd brought combat home with me and took down some very bad people, and I would have done it again. And again. Maybe I was sick in the head, but it was a sickness I had once cherished and now gave in to only occasionally, an addict who could control his addiction, and only used in moderation.

Was Mikki's life in immediate danger? Danger of Second seeing her as a debit now, not an asset, and shooting her up with high-grade H and sending her to a happy land where the destination was that unhappiest of endings?

My gut said she was alive. For now at least. It might have been a father's unrealistic fantasy, but I did not – and this may seem absurd to you – sense that she was dead out there. The exact opposite. Somehow I knew my daughter was breathing and I was determined to keep her that way.

And I knew where I would start.

Right now I was in a pastel sport coat and that wouldn't do. My slacks were tan chinos and that was wrong also, for what I had in mind anyway. In the guest room, I divested myself of those clothes and got into a black polo and black jeans. My sneakers were black also, edged white, and I wasn't exactly a ninja, but close enough for government work.

The .38 was again holstered on my hip, and the box of cartridges bulged in my left jeans pocket. A little tight if I had to get to them quickly, but nothing to do about that. I considered going to the Sidon Wal-Mart, where all sorts of firearms were sold, and buying a few weapons and more rounds of ammo. That meant at least one employee witness and the presence of security cameras.

So the easier and less risky way to upgrade my weaponry would be to take out a few of the enemy and confiscate theirs.

Not that I was entirely sure of who that enemy was.

Yes, my thinking was at once clear and distorted. But I was new at being a father.

In the front room, somebody knocked on the door.

I went out there and the knocking continued. Insistent. The sheer drapes on the window near the door pulsed with red and blue light. I didn't have to peek out to confirm what that was, but I looked anyway, and it was indeed a black-and-white vehicle with the words SIDON POLICE on the white door of the driver, a uniformed officer sitting behind the wheel.

"Mike! Open up!"

Pat.

What the hell was he doing in Sidon?

My hand went to the butt of the holstered .38 on my hip, but didn't stay there long. What was I going to do? Shoot my best friend? Maybe wave the gun at him like he might take the notion seriously that he was in any danger from me?

"Let me in, buddy," he said, his tone of voice easy. "Every cop on Long Island is looking for you. I'm your best option."

I cracked the door, making sure he was alone out there on the stoop, and he was. I opened wider. As was his usual custom, he was in an unfashionable fedora and a brown suit and tie, though he had a generally rumpled look for somebody normally well put together. He had a brown paper bag at his side, like a sack lunch.

What the hell?

"Mind if I come in?" he asked. "We need to talk."

We need to talk. Four of the worst words you could string together in the English language. At least for once it wasn't coming from a female.

"Sure, Pat," I said as genially as I could muster.

I opened the door for him, he stepped inside, pushed his hat back on his blond head, and took the place in as I shut the door behind us.

He asked, "Velda not around?"

"No. You're a little off your beat, aren't you, Pat?"

My cop pal gave me a look that pretended not to study me. "I got called here by the local PD. The NYPD, as a courtesy, brought me in by copter. God, I hate flying in those things."

"A little unnerving," I admitted. "Have a seat?"

His smile was brief and perfunctory. "All right."

We went over to that same couch where the intervention with Mikki had taken place, and where I had rested Velda with her head raised a bit after Second knocked her out with my gun.

Speaking of which.

Before he sat, Pat got into the brown paper sack, which had on it the stenciled-in-black words:

EVIDENCE
CASE FILE #714A
SIDON PD

He withdrew a plastic-bagged item from the paper bag, a most familiar one: a Colt M1911 single-action, recoil-operated, semi-automatic pistol chambered for .45 ACP cartridges.

Mine.

Not necessarily, of course. That could be another well-weathered example of this particular model firearm.

"Yours," Pat said.

"Okay. How did you wind up with it?"

He leaned back. Crossed his arms. "The Sidon Homicide captain entrusted me with it, when he got me on the phone after his computer made an NYPD database match. Lotta hits, Mike. Michael Hammer's Greatest Hits, you might say. It's been fired recently, by the way."

"Not by me, not since that alley we ran down together chasing those dope traffickers."

His expression grew openly skeptical. "I thought you were at the shooting range not long ago. And that's why, if you took a paraffin test, it would clear you."

I grinned. "I sort of lied."

His nod was slow and took a couple of trips. "You sort of lied. I've got a feeling that much is the truth, Mike. Look. I wasn't flown here by copter so two old buddies could have a reunion."

I leaned into where the back cushion met the armrest. I echoed his folded arms. "Why were you coptered in, Pat? Not that I'm not enjoying this reunion."

"You asked me, in my capacity as the head of the Narcotics and Homicide joint task force, to check on Brian Ellis. I believe you made it clear you'd encountered the young man."

"I told you that the last time we talked. He was Mikki's ex. But I have reason to believe I was wrong about him."

I had not told Pat about Mikki's drug use and had no intention of ever doing so.

Now the gray-blue eyes tightened, as if to try to see me more clearly. "Wrong about him, huh? You were seen at an establishment called…" He dug a notebook out of his suitcoat pocket. Flipped to a page. "…Wallace McBeery's. Funny name for a bar today, a yesterday reference like that, but there you are."

"I was struck by it myself. Who remembers Wallace Beery, anyway? Hell of a Pancho Villa though. And before you ask, I was there this afternoon, talking to the Ellis kid."

Those eyes stayed glued on me. "You were seen having an intense conversation. Arguing, perhaps."

"Intense at first. It got… better."

"Did it?"

"Yeah. Damn near friendly."

"When was this?"

"Late afternoon. Maybe four o'clock or a little later. Why?"

His delivery was casual: "Because Brian Ellis was found shot in the alley behind McBeery's."

That hit like a punch.

I asked, "Dead?"

"Brink of. Gut-shot. He's in a coma in the ICU. At Sidon Medical Center."

Small world.

I raised a hand, palm out, as if I was being sworn in. "Not me, Pat. I may have some ideas about who, though."

His voice took on an edge. "Maybe you'd like to share them with me, but first you should know the Sidon PD has its own ideas about the shooter."

"Yeah?"

"Ellis was shot with your .45, Mike. That gun, that old friend of yours, right there."

That's why Second had grabbed it – not to use to clout Velda, though it had come in handy for that purpose, but to fix me for a frame.

Pat's tone shifted into matter-of-fact: "Now you know why the Sidon boys had the NYPD copter me in. Because they figured I was the only cop who could handle you, buddy. The only cop you'd listen to. The friend you would listen to. And come along quietly."

"Do I look like the come-along-quietly type, Pat?"

"Not really. But maybe if I ask nice."

I pointed to the plastic-bagged firearm. "This wasn't me, Pat. I didn't drop the hammer on the Ellis kid. The Sidon cops don't have anybody reporting me getting into it with him at that bar, do they? Or seeing me leaving with him?"

"No," he admitted.

"I was wrong about Ellis. I judged him by how he looked and that same shit judgment had me thinking Second Williams was a short-haired pillar of youth."

Time to ramp it up.

I asked Pat, "You wonder where Velda is?"

"I do."

It might have been a marriage vow – he had loved her once, and probably still did.

So I told him about the scene I'd walked in on, pointing out the brown-red bloodstains on the carpet to his left, just behind him.

And how Velda was in the same hospital as Ellis right now.

"By the way," I said, "if you have that .45 barrel checked for hair and blood residue, you'll find proof of what he did to Velda when he snatched..." I almost said *my daughter*. "...Velda's sister and went God knows where."

His voice was very quiet and had a tremble in it now; he had craned his neck to see the blood-droplet stains and it summoned emotion. "Mike... I ran that check on Ellis that you asked. He came up clean. No arrests even for possession let alone dealing. But I checked the other boy Mikki was seeing, as just a routine matter. What I learned was that Second Williams is suspected of running a small army of dealers all over Long Island on various campuses of high schools and colleges."

I frowned at him. "You might have told me."

"I just learned this a few hours ago, but why would I tell you? So you could play guns and do your cowboy routine here on the Island? I'm working to shut down this syndicate peddling to high school and college kids, and find whoever's above Second, and who's above him. This needs to be a by-the-book operation, not some kill-crazy Mike Hammer spree."

I let my irritation show. "You want to hand me over to the Sidon cops, who'll stick me in a holding cell while Velda's in a hospital room where this Second kid put her?"

"She's in no danger now."

"Are you sure? Velda witnessed Second kidnapping Mikki, and she knows why. You better put a police guard on her room, Pat – put yourself on it, why don't you, and make yourself useful. Or would you rather be responsible for what happens to her?"

That cut him. "Don't, Mike. Don't play that card."

"I'll play whatever card I can lay my hands on. I'll fucking cheat, Pat. You tell the Sidon boys they don't have enough to hold me. Tell 'em you've informed me not to leave the area without first informing them, and that I agreed. And then give me till tomorrow to get Mikki back and give Second Williams the spanking he deserves."

He was shaking his head. "You're an officer of the court, Mike."

"So what? So is any asshole in New York with a P.I. license."

He sat forward. "Well, you rough Second up, you might be the asshole facing charges, with that punk's case thrown out of court. Is that what you want?"

"I want Velda's sister back, safe and sound."

And anybody who's behind this dead and gone.

Out of the corner of my eye, I caught the bagged weapon on the coffee table.

"Pat, how does it happen the Sidon cops got possession of that .45?"

He shrugged. "It was found in that same alley behind McBeery's. Dropped in a garbage can, wiped clean."

My laugh was a harsh thing. "Right. How long have I been carrying that particular rod?"

"You, uh… brought it home from the service."

"How many times do you suppose I've changed barrels on that baby?"

"Half a dozen. More."

"Right. Yet I have a sentimental attachment to it. I like the way it feels in my hand. That rod is part of me. An extension. The garbage is the last place I'd put it – particularly at a murder scene that was my goddamn handiwork. Are you kidding, Pat? This is a frame by an amateur, a punk kid named Garrett Andrew Williams the Second."

Pat sat there thinking, his unblinking eyes looking past me.

"That little prick Second," he said, so quietly it was barely audible, "could have killed Velda, whacking her like that."

"Exactly," I said. "And he might try for real next time."

But Pat seemed on the fence.

"I really should report Mikki missing," he said.

"It hasn't been twenty-four hours, buddy. And that's all I'm asking to find her and bring her home."

Pat folded his arms and leaned back. So many times he'd warned me against taking the law in my own hands when I knew damn well he envied me for pursuing that impulse. I was the id and he was the ego. It had always been that way.

"I can't give you your .45," Pat said. "It's evidence."

"I'll make do," I said.

CHAPTER ELEVEN

The night was cool, not cold, but I was both.

In my makeshift ninja apparel – black polo, black jeans, black trainers, the .38 Police Special in a holster on my left hip, grip out – I was in full combat mode. In foxholes in the Pacific, a few decades and a lifetime ago, I had learned to go into a state of consciousness that was purely reactive, where my only thoughts were processing sounds in the daytime jungle and noise in the nightmare landscape lurking after dark.

Right now it was dark, but with a nearly full moon in a glittering star-flung sky casting a soothing glow of visibility. I'd already thought through what my approach would be. The obvious next step was to confront Garrett Andrew Williams the First. What needed determining right now was whether First was unaware of his son's corrupt activities or was in fact the puppeteer behind them. That would define whether the father was a potential ally or an out-and-out adversary; but either way First ought to be able to point me in Second's direction, specifically to where his son was likely to have taken Mikki to hold her hostage.

The massive two-story tan-brick mansion was bordered by

greenery, thick protective natural walls around the place that might include security devices triggering alarms or cameras that would put me on the screens of a possible surveillance center. Sneaking in, without having surveyed what awaited me, seemed a poor option.

That left a frontal approach.

I pulled the heap down the brick lane through the lushly landscaped grounds, where it wound up in that circular drive around the burbling, bubbling cupid fountain, the front of the manse lit by so much exterior lighting this might have been opening night. That thought was encouraged by the presence of four vehicles, three with New York license plates and another with New Jersey, parked at the curving curb out front, cars that shouted money – a silver Cadillac Eldorado, an olive-hued Lincoln Continental, a deep-purple Ford Thunderbird, a hearse-black Pontiac Gran Prix.

My heap would be the turd in the punch bowl at this party, whatever it was.

I reached in back for my black sports coat and got into it. The weather justified that and the revolver on my hip demanded the concealment it provided. I had already gotten the canvas zippered pouch that was my goodie bag out from under the front seat and onto the rider's side.

Batman had his utility belt and I had my goodie bag.

From it I withdrew a sheathed Ka-Bar knife with a seven-inch blade, three pairs of police handcuffs, a slim black five-inch flashlight, an extra .38 ammo box, my packet of lock picks, roll of silver duct tape, and a six-inch retracted baton (a push button release extending it to just under a foot). The Ka-Bar went on my belt, handcuffs into my right sports coat pocket, the flashlight and ammo box into the left; the baton I clutched in my right hand.

I was about to drop by the Williams place.

First up was getting past the guardian at the gate. I presumed that big Black bruiser was live-in help, and if he wasn't, someone else like him would be. This wasn't all that late to be calling, barely eight o'clock, so my ringing the bell shouldn't have alarmed anyone.

Except maybe its lowlife inhabitants and the company they were entertaining.

Like the postman, I had to ring twice, but eventually the door came halfway open and there he was, that big bald Black butler in a black suit and tie, his face impassive with only the narrowed eyes to express his displeasure. Like the heavyweight boxer he'd once been, George was bigger than humans usually are, and it took no effort from him at all to intimidate.

"I'm here for the meeting," I said. "Running a little late."

He didn't buy it. He shook that big head. In his medium-range baritone, which was deceptively civilized-sounding, he uttered, "Not on my list."

Unless it was his Shit List.

"Check with Mr. Williams," I advised. "He's expecting me."

"Don't think so. You best go."

"You better check with your boss. He won't be happy, you sending me away."

The former boxer was processing that when I brought around the baton that I'd been shielding behind me and clicked the button extending it and whipped it alongside his head.

Despite what you might think, this guy was human and the blow left a slanted red bloody streak along one cheek and encouraged a woozy backward step, which was all I needed to push my way in. I gave him another clout with it, along the other side of his head, and the towering figure went down on one knee. I was ready to clout him again but he fell on his face – I had to get out of the way before the tree of him landed on me.

I shut the door behind me.

The butler in black was face down, not dead or anything, but well and truly visiting the land of fucking Nod. I plucked a Sig Sauer automatic from a shoulder holster under his black jacket and stuck the extra rod in my waistband – a nice opportunity to add a weapon to my limited arsenal.

The hard part was dragging his unconscious ass over to the staircase, seating him below the bottom step to use two handcuffs to secure each of his wrists to separate metal posts of the banister, arms above his head, putting him in a position as awkward as it was humiliating. I duct-taped his mouth shut, too, to add insult to injury, and then bound his ankles together with the stuff. When I was finishing up this operation, he started to come around, and his eyes were getting big with outrage when I gave him another rap alongside the head, raising more wet red and putting the fucker to sleep.

Maybe it killed him. I didn't really care. I'd done my best to leave him with a future and anyway I had more pressing things on my mind.

For a few moments, catching my breath, I stood listening, searching for any sounds on the main floor. The quiet was such that I decided to check out the upper floor first, but all I found was two ridiculously large bathrooms and six bedrooms big as ballrooms, beautifully appointed in a modern way, their gleaming wood floors bearing throw rugs the size of wall maps. One bedroom was decidedly feminine with a blue spread and other tones of blue with an elaborate mirrored vanity; obviously this was where Mrs. First camped out.

No humans, however. Not even any animals, unless you counted the beast handcuffed at the foot of the stairs.

So I tried the main floor, quiet though it had been, and became increasingly afraid the master of the house was away – at his country club, having transported his visitors there for a summit meeting – and found more pointless opulence and needless space by way of a den/family room with a full wall given over to a TV and audio setup; a stainless-steel kitchen; formal dining room; breakfast nook; home office; bathroom you could hold a well-attended orgy in (and maybe from time to time they did); and of course my unaware host's elaborate home gym with wet bar. Most rooms had at least some lights on, so my flashlight had not yet proved necessary.

That's all I can remember to report, other than the general feeling that these rooms were all ridiculously spacious, not a single one you couldn't raise an echo in.

But the notable discovery was that my duct-taped greeter and I were not actually alone in the place. Well, not in the mansion itself, anyway. Of three patios, one was around the pool, which opened off the kitchen (where a few minimal lights were on) by way of double glass doors.

And through those doors I could see – and luckily was not seen, before tucking myself with my back to the wall and my head craned near those double slabs of glass – a meeting in progress. A meeting of the minds – if twisted ones.

In the flaring yellow-orange glow of Tiki torch lamps on poles, five men were seated around the white wrought-iron, beige marble-top table. They sat under the starry sky, the pool their backdrop – a radiant blue with recessed lighting under its surface making a glimmering carpet out of it. Everyone had a mixed drink in front of him and ashtrays were home to cigars and cigarettes.

One of these men, at the far head of the table, was that older variation on Second, his father, wrapped in a paisley brown-and-blue smoking jacket/robe, what might have been pajama bottoms, and sandals; the other four, all angled to look at their host, I recognized, although I had only met one of them. The other three were in the *Daily News* just a little less often than the funnies.

Four wore sports coats in a colorful shade – sky blue, mint green, bright yellow, rust red – apparel with the currently fashionable clownish wide lapels and shirts with pointed collars; slight bell bottoms, too, where I could see them.

These might have been guests at First's country club, or even members – as, like so many men these days, they wore untrimmed sideburns and the kind of long hair they'd probably slapped their sons for wearing a few years ago – and dressed in colors reserved for their wives in the past. None wore ties, though scarves and gold necklaces and even a crucifix were in evidence, but which necks wore what adornment is irrelevant. Let's settle for the following:

In pastel blue we had Gasper Mortelliti.

In pastel green we had Anthony Russo.

In bright yellow we had Carmine Evello.

In rust red we had Maxim Solonik.

See if you can pick the Russian mob boss out of that Sicilian mafioso line-up.

Mortelliti and Russo were seated on my side of the table, Evello and Solonik on the far side. At the head, down to the right, sat Garrett Andrew Williams the First.

Positioned protectively were a pair of nameless hoods, nameless to me anyway – one with his back partially to the double doors, so very close to where I'd snugged myself against a wall; another between the pool and Evello and Solonik on the table's far side. Mine looked Italian, the other Russian, but I'm just guessing. These apparent bodyguards sported leisure suits, the Italian in blue, the Russian (appropriately) in light red… you might call it pink. Maybe he was confident in his masculinity.

Though not exactly the United Nations, this was nonetheless a significant gathering of ethnic groups. All but Williams wore the kind of faces the lighting made grotesque angular masks out of. These pastel pricks could have posed for a sculptor fashioning gargoyles.

I could hear Garrett Andrew Williams the First conveying his vision of the future.

"What my son has undertaken," he was saying, "at my behest, gentlemen, demonstrates a pattern we can duplicate at high schools and particularly on college campuses. I intend to continue using my gifted boy on further college New York State campuses over the next several years – he can transfer from one school to another, creating small armies of dealers wherever he goes. This same approach can be undertaken in virtually every state of our great country."

Bullet-headed Mortelliti, whose skeptical look suggested he found even the milk from his mother's tit suspect, said, "I would feel better, Williams, if your boy was here. His insights into this distribution scheme would be worth hearing."

"I know, I know," Williams said placatingly, patting the air with a palm, "and he wanted to be. Business called Second away unexpectedly, and we all know business comes first. He has a Phi Beta Kappa mind, my son."

"Vot kind uv brain?" the square-headed Russian asked, squinting at his host.

White hair threaded black, skull so narrow it might have been squeezed at birth, Evello said, "He means the kid is smart. I dealt with Second. That's what they call the boy. Sharp as a tack."

"It's a good move," Russo said, nodding. "Jersey is in."

"Speaking for the six families," Evello said, "it makes a lot of sense. But we roll out gradual. Don't want too much attention all at once."

"Let it be a social problem," Mortelliti said, a smart man, if not Phi Beta Kappa. "Something to blame on the fuckin' hippies."

"Our experience," Williams said, with a smarmy smile, "is that someone clean-cut like my boy attracts little attention. All these damn freaks and SDS types running around campus will take the heat… and give us a lot of business."

That got a general laugh out of the group.

I slid a door open and stepped out onto the patio with the Ka-Bar in my left hand and the .38 in my right, edging behind the apparent Italian hood and putting the blade of the Ka-Bar to his throat. The bodyguard stiffened and blurted, "Jesus fuck!" in half-prayer, half-surprise. He smelled of Old Spice – easier than bathing, I guess.

All faces turned toward me and eyes were wide and mouths open and down-turned, emitting various cries of anger and alarm, mostly in English, but some Sicilian and Russian in there too, a polyglot of outrage.

"I won't start killing people unless I have to," I said. "Here's what I want."

"Fuck you, Hammer!" Evello said, but it lacked confidence.

"Everybody put any hardware you got on the table," I said, ignoring the mob boss's outburst. "By the grip with two fingers, please. Includes little-girl pocket guns. If you got an ankle piece to get rid of, tell me first. Suspicious moves make me... suspicious."

Nothing.

"*Now*, gentlemen, or I cut a throat and start shooting."

Guns clunked onto the table.

The bodyguard standing behind the seated Evello and Solonik got his weapon out from under his arm – like him, the gun was Russian, a Makarov – and he played by my rules, removing it from its underarm holster with two fingers...

...but swiveled it into his grasp and fired toward me, hitting and spider-webbing a glass door to my left. With the .38 in my right hand, I returned fire, and the head shot misted red as the Russian thug fell backward into the pool as with my left I cut the other bodyguard's throat and blood sprayed the men at the table, dotting them like some disease broke out, and maybe it had because every one of them grabbed for the gun they'd just politely laid on the table and Mortelliti and Russo scattered to the right, toward the white-curtained poolside

cabana. *I picked the runners off like ducks on the fly, head shots that made red fireworks and they tumbled into the pool and made a splash.*

Meanwhile Evello and Solonik collaborated in upending the table to take cover behind, but the marble top shattered and exposed them, and as they crouched to return fire, they were suddenly unprotected and took head shots as well, ribboning spurts of scarlet not mist, tumbling backward and joining the others in the water.

I moved toward Garrett Andrew Williams the First, who was cowering behind his white, blood-spattered wrought-iron chair, which made pitiful cover. But he had managed to stay out of the line of fire, smart enough not to grab for any of the guns when things had gotten abruptly real.

"Have a seat, Garrett," I said.

He rose slowly and settled himself in the wrought-iron chair and I pulled one over. Dead men floated on their faces nearby like huge grotesque pastel flowers with shimmering scarlet stems.

"Where's the girl?" I asked him. Businesslike. Almost casual. "Where does your boy have her?"

Flecked with blood spray, Williams replied in a fear-soaked tremble. "He's going to call you. You should go home. Sit by the phone. He'll call."

"And set something up to trade the girl for... what?"

"Your... your willingness to drop this whole thing."

"Does that seem likely to you?"

"Second didn't anticipate... any... any of *this*..."

He gestured to the lit-from-beneath pool and the corpses bobbing there.

"It'll be a trap, of course," I said.

"No! No, he'll be a... an honest broker in this. He'll exchange the girl for you just agreeing to, to... fade away."

"Not how it's going to be," I said. "You're going to tell me, Garrett, where your son is holding her. Or you're going to join your guests for a nighttime swim."

"All right... all right..."

I heard crunching on glass behind me, and whirled from the chair and dropped into a crouch.

The Black protector of the Williams estate had staggered onto the patio through the kitchen and his massive form seemed to dwarf all else, his wrinkled black suit making a ghastly undertaker out of him, his wrists each bearing a loose handcuff, ragged duct tape trailing off his legs, his expression narrow-eyed, open-mouthed rage, and in his right hand was a nine-millimeter semi-auto handgun that looked like a toy prop in that immense mitt.

I think the only reason the heavyweight paused before shooting was how close his employer and I were to each other, and that half-second was enough for me to fire a round that caught him in the throat, his hands rising there with the dangling handcuffs like terrible jewelry, the automatic dropping to the tile floor, the gurgling coming from him like a drain taking on water. Then that huge frame staggered back and the spider-webbed glass door finally shattered and he went through it and crashed to the floor in a discordant crackling as the mighty carcass met glass fragments.

Garrett the First threw himself toward the puzzle pile of broken marble where various handguns belonging to dead gangsters were mixed in, and grabbed a gun and was on his back looking up at me, pointing the late Solonik's Makarov when reflexively I shot him in his left eye.

Didn't take long at all for the remaining orb to film over.

"Shit," I said, getting on my feet.

The host of the party lay in a pile of marble chunks and firearms and spilled drinks and spilled blood with his paisley robe serving as an insufficient shroud and I was fucked. Fucked!

"Buy you a drink?" a female voice asked.

I whirled, .38 in hand, and at the white-curtained mouth of the cabana stood my late host's wife, Tammy Williams, her hands up, palms out; she looked cool and lovely in a form-fitting red-and-white sarong and red kitten heels. There hadn't been any fear in her voice, but her eyes said something else.

"I'd prefer you not kill me, Mike," she said. "I was just the bartender here. Garrett insisted I stay away from the meeting itself."

I crossed the patio to her, skirting the bodies of the bodyguard whose throat I'd slit and the fallen heavyweight whose fingers at his throat still oozed blood. My .38 remained in hand, but lowered some.

"I could use a beer," I said.

An eyebrow lifted casually over one of those money-green eyes. "All I have is imported. Lowenbrau? Light or dark?"

"Dark."

Then we were sitting again at the little bar in the cabana. She brought me the bottle of beer from the mini fridge on a shelf lined with liquor behind the counter, then came around and took the stool next to me. She didn't want me to think maybe she had a gun back there.

"You don't seem too upset," I said, "you're a widow now."

She was having a Lowenbrau, too. "Not at all. My husband's passing nullifies the portion of my pre-nup that's been hanging over me. The only way I inherit anything is if Garrett goes first. And thanks to you, he has."

I swigged the beer, studied the lovely cold face. "And where does that leave you?"

Her smile was slight, her gesture large. "This house is not mortgaged. The sale of it will fund me nicely, probably for the rest of my life. And there's money in the bank, several banks, actually. You've done me the greatest favor anyone ever has, Mike... unless you kill me, too, of course."

"Of course. But why would I?"

Her bare shoulders above the red-and-black of the sarong shrugged. "Well, I *am* a witness. But then, what exactly did I witness? Seems to me what I saw was a falling out among, shall we call them, thieves? Which got rather out of hand? I was lucky enough to survive by hiding in here. Who knows exactly what happened after that?"

"Then you want no part of Garrett's business?"

She made a face, shook her head. Blonde hair bounced. "No! No. I want nothing to do with any of his business dealings, or practices. Oh, I might refurbish that country club of his. He's been using it as a tax dodge for years, deducting improvements and renovation that never took place. It's a money laundry with bad carpet."

She put on a phony sad face.

"I *did* lie to you about one thing, when we spoke earlier, Mike."

"Oh?"

Tammy seemed embarrassed to admit it as she said, "Garrett and I hadn't slept together in years. You see, his gate swung both ways, as they say… but as he got older, he only preferred swinging it in a direction that didn't include me, or frankly any female. Got obsessed with body building… and builders. I've lived a lie for over a decade, Mike, that has been at once cushy and a damn nightmare… Another Lowenbrau?"

"Better hold it to one."

Was she stringing me along? Improvising a story that might save her life? Or keep me here till the cops showed up?

"I should probably be going," I said, lifting off the stool.

She gently guided me back down. "No rush. We have no neighbors nearby. This is a seven-acre estate, after all. Your little shooting match wasn't heard by anyone but the participants. And me. You probably already figured that."

"You won't use the phone the moment I leave?"

Her smile was as confident as it was beautiful. "Of course not. Oh, I'll make a call in half an hour or so, when I tell them my story – the one you and I concocted. And when you're long away."

"I'd like to believe you."

She put a hand on my thigh. "What would it take, Mike? I don't believe you're in a romantic mood right now. A raincheck? Unless your kink is doing it among the recently dead."

"No. I'm the least kinky guy around. Just your average boring joe."

"That secretary of yours is lucky to have you." Tammy smiled on one side and lifted an eyebrow on the other. "How about I tell you where you're likely to find Second and the missing girl? How would that rate as a show of good faith?"

"Just fine."

She sighed, as if a difficult negotiation had just transpired; and maybe it had.

"The family has a cottage," she said. "Nothing terribly fancy, just a place Garrett used to take the rabble he'd pick up in bars or at some gym. All very distasteful. Oh, I have nothing against alternate lifestyles. But not when it's my husband."

"I can see that. Where is this cottage?"

Tammy raised a red-nailed forefinger. "I'll tell you. I'll write it down."

She utilized a notepad and pencil on the counter nearby.

As she wrote, I said, "I guess you have no maternal instinct toward Second."

She tore the little sheet of paper off the pad. "Not at all. He's a vile young man... and due to inherit half the estate. But if something happened to him..."

"Something could," I admitted.

Tammy leaned close; stroked my cheek. "I hope you don't think I'm a terrible person, Mike."

"Even if I did, I think you'd get over it."

She backed away a little, laughing. "Disappointed I'm not the femme fatale in all of this?"

I shrugged. "Well, from your stepson's point of view, you kind of are. You're doing fine with me as long as you stick to the story that you hid when all the carnage went down. That I was never here tonight."

She opened both hands and shrugged. "You never were. Sure you won't have one for the road, Mike?"

CHAPTER TWELVE

Night provided a searchlight of a moon aided by enough stars to turn the blacktop I was heading down into a glowing pathway. Driving alone at night is the kind of solitary endeavor that creates a state almost other-worldly. If there isn't much traffic, encountering the occasional car or especially truck can somehow be a shock to the system.

Still, you could really drive on a night like this. Just drive, going nowhere in particular. Who was it who said that? Mr. Toad in *Wind in the Willows*, wasn't it? No willows in sight but plenty of wind stirred by the heap, with greenery at left, little dwellings at right dotting a dark brown beach and facing a deep blue, shimmering navy surface sporting a vertical band of reflected moonlight. It would be restful under other circumstances.

Not these.

Only half an hour ago, more or less, I had left the scene of carnage at the mansion to follow the directions provided by the newly minted widow Williams. I slowed, pulled over, and parked the heap just off the blacktop, with a wooded area on my left and one small cottage after another at my right stretching endlessly to the horizon. But the cottage I'd be visiting, Second's stepmother had assured me, would be quiet and secluded.

I stayed within the various birch, oak, and pine trees bordering the curving crushed-rock lane, embracing the dark, approaching with the dead butler's Sig Sauer from the Williams meeting, having left my untraceable .38 to add to the forensics confusion. Twigs and leaves and brush underfoot, and branches blocking my path, meant taking my time, to prevent announcing my arrival. So some stealth was required, however much urgency flowed within me knowing my daughter – *my daughter!* – was in peril.

Such a silly word, peril. Old-fashioned. Even quaint. And yet in this case so very apropos. I continued trooping slowly through the nighttime jungle, part of me on Long Island with its Atlantic, part of me on Guadalcanal in the Pacific. The night might be cool, but those were sweat droplets on my face.

Not a good time for a malaria flare-up, Mike, I told myself. *And you with no quinine pills to pop.*

Then, there it was – the Williams cottage, perched on a modest rise, which would no doubt provide a nice high view of the beach and the bay without any ticky-tacky cottages in the way. Nestled there among all this greenery, bathing in ivory nighttime, the boxy structure wore gray rustic siding and a matching shingle roof. Nothing much distinctive about it…

…except the gleaming gold Corvette pulled in at the foot of the wooden stairs up to the front door of this modestly elevated retreat.

Oddly, the place was a rough-hewn echo of the Sterling bungalow back in Sidon. As I moved in closer, I stayed within the surrounding trees and brush, stopping toward the rear of the cottage, where the foliage trailed off in a sandy slope toward the blacktop and the brown beach and the deep blue of the bay.

Second, of course, knew nothing of what had gone down at the Williams homestead, or at least that much seemed likely. My take was the junior Williams had shot Brian Ellis in the McBeery's alley and dumped my .45 in a trash can there, setting in motion what Second surely thought would be an inevitable process ending with the local cops tossing my ass in the clink.

The boy's father had shown no indication of worry about running into me either, and had gone on with his drug-racketeer confab as planned. My guess was it'd been the father behind the machinations designed to get me out of the game – that he'd advised his son to shoot Ellis and credit me for it. Second had been sent, or perhaps had decided himself, to spirit Mikki to this cottage to hold as a bargaining chip, should I somehow wriggle out of the frame-up.

Sometimes having Captain Pat Chambers of Homicide for a best friend comes in handy.

A modest deck ran around the house, lengthened only on the bay side to accommodate some wooden picnic-style furniture. What I had in mind would be no picnic at all. I went up the handful of steps onto this back deck, my pistol at the ready, boardwalk-type planking groaning slightly underfoot. Then I took a cautious tour around the house, looking in windows.

At the front of the house was a living room, modern furnishings and pine paneling, a cozy mini-hunting-lodge effect. And on the living room couch, Second, wearing a fresh floral shirt and white jeans and sky-blue trainers, stretched lazily out, smoking a joint, a half-empty dime bag of grass on the floor nearby. So clean-cut with his short blond hair and lithely muscular frame, though his face bore the bruised battering Ellis gave him, even if the swelling had gone down. On his lap, folded open, was a paperback edition of *The Electric Kool-Aid Acid Test*. On the floor next to him was a little silver, walnut-gripped Mauser .22.

On the left side of the house was a homey kitchen where Betty Crocker might have vacationed; and in back of that, a bedroom with framed hunting prints, an apparent guest room. A windowless door off the deck appeared to belong to a hallway; at the rear was a bedroom, and beyond it a TV den. But what was most significant was that other bedroom, which was all gray and ebony with an occasional faux Picasso print, perfect for a romantic fling with either male or female.

And on the bed with its light gray spread lay Mikki, in a near-naked sprawl, skimpy white bra and sheer panties, her long hair fanning out like seaweed. The all-those-years-ago image of Velda, her wrists bound and her lovely naked body hanging from a rafter, blazed in my brain, a horrific fire that would never go out. Mikki looked so much like her mother. Too much, right now.

No one would take what the girl was doing as sleeping – she was in a deep druggy state, her left arm extended like Christ on the cross, only that wasn't stigmata, it was needle tracks.

How to deal with Second?

I was tempted.

I won't lie to you. I was tempted to just elbow-shatter the glass of a living room window and shoot that privileged little prick between his bloodshot eyes. That would've been doing him a favor, considering the tragedy awaiting him at home – put him out of his misery.

After all, wasn't he an orphan?

Or I could just ignore him and go through a bedroom window or even the front door, knock him out and tie him up, or if he gave me any trouble, plug him then and there. Maybe he was too zonked out of his mind right now to do much about anything I might be up to.

I wasn't anxious to kill a kid, no matter how big a baby drug kingpin he might be.

As I got out the lock-pick packet, selected two tools and began work on the rear deck door there in the moonlight, I mulled the situation. Possibly I could find Mikki's clothes, help her into them, and walk her out the back way, through the rear deck door. Carry her out, if need be, but doing that would risk alerting her bad choice for a boyfriend on that couch.

The picks did their work and the back door opened quietly.

Sig Sauer in my right hand, barrel raised, I crept up the hallway into the masculine bedroom where the feminine child lay in something like, but not really, sleep.

"Mikki," I whispered, "it's Mike."

Nothing.

"We have to get you out of here, honey," I whispered.

She stirred.

I slipped an arm around her bare waist and helped her off the bed. "Come on, baby. Come on."

But her feet weren't working, at least not yet, and a noise toward the front of the place had me setting her back down on the bed, her eyelids fluttering like butterflies while I slipped carefully into the hall, Sig Sauer pointing straight out now.

No further noise.

I made my way slowly toward the living room, listening intently, and I could see the back of that couch where presumably Second still lounged, and as I entered the room he stepped out from the wall to my left and I wheeled toward him as he grinningly pointed his little .22 at me.

Figuring he might hesitate before firing, I squeezed the trigger on the butler's Sig Sauer... *and the fucking thing jammed!*

Second reacted, blue eyes popping in that battered mask of a face, but still he didn't fire, and I threw the gun at him and caught him on the forehead. The gouge bled and red began trickling down into his eyes, affecting his vision enough to keep him from firing accurately, though he did finally fire, twice, the .22s sounding like explosions in the small pine-paneled room, wild shots that flew right by me but made my ears ring and I dove for him and took him down onto the floor, with a resounding *whump*, but he – we – rolled onto a throw rug, which we both scooted on, taking a short, slippery ride.

Normally I could have knocked him out with one punch, but he was on top and my leverage was limited, and he still had that .22 in hand and before doing anything else, I'd have to wrestle it free first, and with a double grip around his wrist I shook and shook, making fingers out of his fist, the loosened grasp freeing the weapon, which hit the floor and spun a ways away.

While he scrambled like a spider after that gun, I quickly scooped up the Sig Sauer and opened the action, removed the clip, racked the slide till the jammed round flew out, then put the clip back and racked the slide again.

Second got to his feet, with the .22 again in hand, his blond beach boy persona spoiled by a sneer, but that sneer dissolved when he realized I was up too, pointing the pistol at him again, in a pure Mexican stand-off.

"Your gun jammed," he said, giving me and the Sig Sauer a skeptical look. He had the .22 trained on me.

"I cleared it," I said. "Should work fine now."

"Maybe not."

I shrugged. "Maybe not. Care to see?"

Turns out I was the bandito and he was the gringo, because looking into the fathomless barrel of a Sig Sauer changed his mind about trading bullets with me. I guess my reputation preceded me.

Second raised his hands, one of which still held the .22, and grinned again, but in a shit-eating way now, and said, "I'll drop the gun, okay? No funny business?"

"I don't know. I can always use a good laugh. Uh, toss it gentle. These things are known to go off."

He nodded and pitched the gun, easily, to the floor by the door.

"Step away from the gun," I said.

Second did as he was told.

"None of this was my idea," he said, rather apologetically, "if it matters. My dad thought having Mike Hammer nosing around was bad for his business. Can you blame him?"

"I'm generous with placing blame. You get some, too, Second."

His hands were still up. "Look, I'm the smallest fry there is – a dealer on a college campus."

"With aspirations."

He shrugged, risked a smile. "Maybe. But at my age and with my... pedigree? If I got caught at it, it'd be slap-on-the-wrist time. You know that."

I shook my head slowly. "Not when you go around kidnapping young women."

He thought a bit before responding to that. "You'd have to be willing to expose her bad habit, shall we say, to the press. Be quite an embarrassment for the family, not to mention Mikki herself. She might have trouble getting into a decent college, after. She'd never be able to pick up the pieces of her tennis-star dreams."

"Got it figured out, do you?"

Now he was grinning again. "I'm Phi Beta Kappa all the way, Hammer."

"I heard that. What was Mikki to you, Second? How does she figure into this?"

The question seemed to surprise him. "She's a customer. And, well... she's... a customer."

"What were you *going* to say, Second?"

"Nothing."

"A nice piece of ass? Is that what you were going to say?"

His smile seemed to curdle. "You can't kill a guy for that."

"Oh, I think I could."

And now his smile was gone entirely.

"Go ahead and put your hands down," I said, almost friendly. He did.

I went on: "I'm gonna give you a break, Second. I'm prepared to let you walk away from this... on two conditions."

"I'm listening."

"You're going home to a real mess."

His eyes tightened. "What are you talking about?"

"You'll see. No need to go into it now. But you're to keep me out of the aftermath. *And* Mikki. We weren't part of your business plans, or disrupting them. Understood?"

"I guess. But *what mess?*"

"No. Say it."

"Understood."

I gave him the nastiest look I have, and that's saying something. "Because if you bring me into this, if you bring Mikki into this, some morning you are not going to wake up. The *New Yorker* will do an article called 'The Short, Happy Life of Garrett Andrew Williams the Second.' Got it?"

He had gone a little pale. "I got it, Mr. Hammer."

Now he got my best smile. "I like that. We're back to 'Mister' Hammer. The other thing – the second thing, Second. You're going to help me get Mikki out of here. You've got her clothes somewhere, right?"

"Right."

"We'll get her dressed and out to your car. Then you'll drive us to where I'm parked and we'll be on our way and you'll be on yours."

I gestured toward the hallway.

But Second stayed put. "What did you mean, I'm going home to a 'real mess?'"

"Discussing that's not on the menu. You'll have plenty of time for that."

Obviously not thrilled with my response, he stopped at the bathroom to wash the blood from his face, under my supervision of course. Then, under my gun again, he took the lead down the hallway to the male bedroom where the female waited. She was sitting up now. On the edge of the bed. Not that she looked great or anything – she was pale and wan and damn near haggard.

Her clothes were under her bed – the same ones she'd worn this afternoon, a hundred years ago: baby-blue sweater, pink bellbottoms, but dirt-smudged and wrinkled. Even the open-toed sandals looked scuffed. We helped her into them. Second behaved himself. He was almost gentle with her.

Helping her pull the long-sleeved sweater up over her needle-ravaged arm made me cringe.

Mikki spoke for the first time since I'd shown up on the scene. Her voice was soft with a sandpaper edge. To Second, she said, "I need something."

Second said, "You're not a customer anymore."

Mikki said to me, "Mike. I need something."

"You need help, kid," I said. "And I'm going to get it for you. I promise."

She slumped, but she was awake.

I directed him to walk her out, with me behind them, Sig Sauer in hand. That proved to be a mistake.

In the living room, he shoved her at me, virtually flung her, and a pile of Mikki, a ragdoll of a girl, took me down unintentionally, the Sig Sauer flying. I couldn't be gentle, no time for that – I pushed her off me and went for him, tackled him to the floor, and I was on top of the bastard, ready to cave his face in with a fist, when he stuck the nose of the .22 in my belly, that gun he'd retrieved from near the front door where earlier he'd dropped it.

"Get off me, Hammer."

Through my teeth I said, "No 'Mister?'"

"Get the hell off me!"

I eased off him. Rose.

He motioned for me to get away from him, clutching the .22 in both hands. He backed up to the front door, that golden Corvette waiting behind it like a game show prize. "You underestimated me, Hammer. Bad mistake. I'm taking you out of the game before you hurt my father and me any more than you already have."

I only had one card left to play.

I worked up a sneer of a smile. "That mess you have waiting at home, Second?"

A moment of confused interest colored his frown. "Yeah?"

"Your father's dead," I said, each word a distinct bullet. "So are all his partners. Even your fucking butler bought it. Courtesy of me."

It was a risk. I thought it would unhinge him enough for me to make a play. Give me the second I needed from the Second I knew.

But all it did was bring his hands clutching that .22 high and aimed right at my head. Maybe I should say my stupid head…

The gunshot thundered.

But it only shook Second like the naughty child he was before the trickle of blood over his heart watered the floral shirt and his mouth was in rah-rah fashion when he flopped onto his face, the front door splattered with a bloody bunch of him that was sliding down like a big bug had hit it.

I turned to see Mikki angled behind me with that Sig Sauer in her hand – this time it hadn't jammed – wearing the coldest damn expression I ever saw on anybody, this side of a mirror. The lovely girl in soiled sweater and bellbottoms was momentarily steady before falling and getting caught by her father before anything else bad could happen to her.

CHAPTER THIRTEEN

Everyone thinks of twilight as following sunset; but there's a morning twilight, too, and as I stood snatching a smoke under the overhang outside the Sidon Medical Center ER entry, I watched the blue sky sneaking up to assert itself. I'd just tossed the butt trailing sparks into what was left of the night, promising myself to quit again, when the red light of an ambulance pulled in, flashing but not accompanied by a siren.

Though such an occurrence was hardly unusual under these circumstances, I thought I knew what this was, and I was right. Dr. Larry Snyder stepped from the rider's-side seat, leaving a white-uniformed attendant at the wheel, to pull his vehicle over to one side should a more pressing case arrive before the expected passenger could be loaded in to this one.

The Snyder Clinic's honcho was a slender guy with a pleasant if nondescript face, his black-rimmed glasses going well with his black hair, though some silver was working the sideburns. Jesus, even Larry was wearing them long and bushy like the kids these days. Could it be I was out of step?

Hell, no. The world was out of step with me.

From Larry's black suit and crisp red-and-black striped tie, you'd never know I'd woken him at his private number and that he'd got out of bed to drive here from upstate New York and do a favor for a friend.

We shook hands.

"How's the girl?" he asked. His voice had a professorly midrange tone.

"You tell me. They've still got her in a triage bed in the ER ward."

We entered through automatic sliding doors into the usual stark white world of the Emergency Room. Pretty quiet right now, no patients awaiting admission, any relatives off in a private area, and the two nurses behind the counter exhibiting that combo of weary and bored that comes near end of shift.

Nonetheless, the admitting nurse knew to expect Dr. Snyder's arrival and made a call summoning the medic on duty, which was the same female doc with the Elsa Lanchester hair who I'd spoken to not so long ago. A thousand years back.

She was expecting us, too, and led the way. Larry fell in with me.

"I'll make a preliminary exam and get this in motion," he said. "You'll be going along, I trust."

"Yeah. Just so this isn't an elaborate trick designed to dry me out again."

That amused him, though part of him seemed to take it seriously. "Why, Mike? Did you fall off the wagon?"

"No, but I thought about it." As we walked, I put a hand on his shoulder. "Listen, I'll be up at Velda's room." I gave him the number. "Just want to see how she's doing. If the docs approve, she may make the ride with us."

"She *is* very close to her sister," he said with a knowing nod.

"Close as it gets," I said.

I found Velda just finishing up her breakfast on a tray that swung out from the little bedside stand. She looked damn good for a babe out of make-up with one side of her skull bandaged.

"You look like you have a story to tell," Velda said, raising an eyebrow.

"I do, as long as nobody but you is listening."

"My doctor's already been around. Shoot. If that isn't too dangerous a suggestion to make to Mike Hammer."

I stood close at her bedside, leaning in, and gave her confidential chapter and verse. Judging by her facial reactions, she might have been watching a horror movie.

After I wrapped it up, she gave a long sigh. "Oh, what our girl has gone through."

"About that."

"Yes?"

I locked eyes with her. "I haven't told Mikki. I had other things on my mind, like wiping down anything I might have touched at that cottage."

"Always a good practice after a killing," she said dryly.

"So what do you think?" I asked.

"What do *you* think, Mike?"

Now it was my turn to sigh. "It's a little late in the day for me to be a good father. To drive her and a date to the senior prom. To give her away at the altar to some lucky bum."

Velda reached out and took my hand and squeezed it. "It's your call, Mike. Really, I had no business keeping it from you, for all these years. Can you… can you ever forgive me?"

"Oh, hell, I already have."

The big brown eyes were swimming with tears, but she didn't let them loose. It wasn't her way. I was the sentimental slob between the two of us. Oddly, I was dry-eyed – what I'd been through the long night before had a dulling effect.

"Doll, you had good reason to keep the truth from me. You couldn't know if I'd be a blackout drunk one day or a psycho blasting bad guys on another, like the Lone fucking Ranger."

Her mouth turned up at the corners. "I didn't mind being your Tonto."

I summoned a grin. "I always suspected those two fooled around, after dark by the campfire. No, baby, listen. You may not have noticed, but I've made my share of enemies over the years."

"And more than your share of friends." She squeezed my hand again. "You don't have an impressive record of taking on paying clients when there's some windmill to chase."

I huffed a laugh. "Now I'm Don Quixote."

"Which makes me Sancho Panza, doesn't it?"

"I always wondered about *those* two, too." I slung a hip up onto the side of her bed, with a squeak. "No, and who's to say what windmill I might go chasing after next? Only they aren't, they've *never* been, imaginary foes. It's been real dragons, not windmills posing as any. They've left me beaten to a pulp or in burning buildings or shot half to pieces, and they have grudges. I'm not the only guy going after payback, you know. Who insists on getting even."

"And then some," she admitted.

"No, let's leave it that way."

Her expression turned curious. "Leave it... what way?"

I shrugged. "You're Mikki's sister. I'm her godfather, her 'Uncle Mike.' Let her live a normal life. A *safe* life. Safer, anyway."

Velda's expression darkened. "Mikki will always know, though, won't she?"

"Know...?"

"That she took a life."

I shrugged again, more elaborately this time. "Hell, doll, I don't know if she'll even remember it. It may be a bad dream she relives in the middle of the occasional long night. Small price to pay for saving her old man's life. Even if she doesn't know that's whose life she saved. Even if... she can't ever know it."

Those big brown eyes held onto mine for a long, long time.

Then she said, "That's your decision, Mike?"

I slipped off the bed onto my two feet. "No, it has to be our decision."

She thought about that. "Our decision."

"You okay with it?"

Her soft hand and their soft fingertips found my unshaven cheek. "I'm okay with it, darling."

I kissed the hand and gave it back to her. "Hey, don't forget. We aren't married yet. You had that kid out of wedlock. Surely you don't wanna come clean and make a little bastard out of her, do ya?"

That made her laugh, hard enough to raise a hand toward her bandage, then lower it. "Mike... you and Larry Snyder, you're going to convey Mikki to that rehab clinic of his, right? Like, right now?"

"That's the plan."

She gestured around her; the monitoring gizmo still beeped. "Well, they've had me under observation all night. I think I can get them to discharge me… if necessary, sign my care over to Dr. Snyder. Can you try to make that happen?"

"Absolutely. That female medic of yours? I think she's got the hots for me. I'll go wrap her around my little finger."

I kissed her forehead, gently, and headed out.

But I was still at the door when she called out: "Mike?"

"Yeah, doll?"

"I love you," she said.

"I love *you*, baby."

I told you I was a sentimental slob.

EPILOGUE

Nobody was left at the graveside but Pat and me, the two men who had loved her.

When I wrote my cases up for book publication, I left some things out. Nothing was omitted to make me look better, I assure you. Nobody in these accounts comes off worse than me except maybe those I liquidated, as the spooks would put it. Velda's last name was one thing I left out of these accounts for the longest time, till she herself complained.

"Even Jane in the Tarzan books had a last name," she said once.

"What was it?" I'd asked her.

"Well... I don't remember. But she had one."

"Porter."

"What?"

"Jane Porter," I said. "Till she changed it to Greystoke."

She laughed and shook her head, the silver-tinged raven arcs swinging. "The damnedest things stick to that brain of yours, Mike."

I held my hands out, palms up. "You want your name in the books, baby, you got it."

And there it was, chiseled in granite –

VELDA STERLING-HAMMER

— and the pun scolded me: too often, in those first years, I had taken her for granted. But that was the early days. After those seven years she was away, doing the CIA's bidding in the wretched Soviet Union, I knew what a treasure I had in this woman. What a partner.

And now the best part of me was gone.

Lucky for the world, at least the evil shits in it, that I was an old man now. Or they'd be sleeping with one eye open.

"Quite a story," Pat said.

We'd been standing in the gentle, almost tropical breeze on a gray day that should have felt colder, me telling Pat about those weeks in Long Island... even the bullets that had flown at that drug-lord confab at the Williams place and how I'd rescued Mikki from the clutches of that seemingly clean-cut short-haired beach boy of a villain at the bay cottage.

I left out only that Mikki had pulled the trigger on Second, taking for myself the credit and blame. Probably dangerous to be admitting such blatantly illegal things to a police inspector, even a retired one like Pat Chambers.

But not really.

The only friend of mine who had rivaled Pat was Jack Williams, who had given his arm to keep a Jap bayonet from ending me, and who had in common with Garrett Andrew Williams the First and Second only a surname. But even Jack faced stiff competition from Captain Chambers who had covered for me, and covered *up* for me, and had so often had my back in the "peacetime" combat my surly disposition had embraced like a sweet sickness.

"I know you need some time alone with her," Pat said, and, impulsively, he hugged me – the only time I remember him doing that – and slapped his fedora back on and walked off into the gray afternoon.

"See you later, Pat," I said.

Didn't Randolph Scott say that once?

To Joel McCrea?

We spent just a few minutes together, Velda and I, and what I had to say, and what I imagined she said to me, is really none of your business.

And then I wasn't alone.

No, it wasn't Velda's ghost... but almost.

She was at my side, the lovely girl – no, make that *woman* – who was my daughter, and looked at me questioningly.

"You talked to your friend," Mikki said, "a long time."

"I guess. Maybe I figure the longer I stay here, the longer she's still with us."

"She'll always be with us. You know that."

Behind us, at a respectful distance, in a dark suit and sunglasses and a trim beard, was Mikki's husband of over twenty-five years. I admit I lost count. Today Brian Ellis ran motorcycle dealerships all around the east coast out of his Long Island headquarters.

I turned to look at her; Mikki was right there next to me.

"She was your mother, you know," I said.

As casual as *Pass the salt.*

"I know," she said.

I swallowed. "So I guess you know how I figure in this, too."

Her big so-familiar deep brown eyes locked onto me. "I've known for a long time."

It came like a gentle slap. But a slap nonetheless.

I asked, "Then why—"

"It needed to come from you."

So now, as if that gray sky had come down low enough to threaten crushing me, I had decades to explain to this woman, all at once. I did my best.

I said, "I've made a lot of enemies in my time, kitten. I couldn't have you out there on the firing line. And, anyway... it was her wish. Her call. She made me promise. It's really just about all she ever asked of me."

Only curiosity, not judgment, colored her expression. "And yet... all these years... you kept your word to her, didn't you?"

"I did."

She held her hand out to me. No black gloves to go with the mourning weeds. Her fingers were long and graceful and her grasp... it was so warm.

"Walk me," she said.

We turned and started away.

Her husband nodded to me before falling in behind us. I walked her out of the cemetery toward where cars in the parking lot waited to take us away from all the death. For now.

"You kept it in you," she said. "All these years."

"I did," I admitted.

"How could you?" she asked.

"It wasn't easy," I said.

TIP OF THE FEDORA

My continuing thanks to Titan Books publishers Nick Landau and Vivian Cheung, and their editorial staff, in particular chief operating officer Andrew Sumner, who remains the ideal editor for Mickey Spillane and me; my gratitude to all of them for their dedication for pursuing – and completing – the Mickey Spillane's Mike Hammer Legacy Project.

This is the final novel planned from material in the late Mickey Spillane's voluminous files. The non-Hammer novels we've published (and a few more of these may yet happen) are due to editor Charles Ardai, the co-founder of Titan's sister company, Hard Case Crime. For the record, these books include *Dead Street* (2007), *The Consummata* (2011*)*, and *The Last Stand* (2018).

Mrs. Mickey Spillane – Jane Spillane – has made these efforts possible; our thanks to her for her always welcome encouragement and support. My wife, writer Barbara Collins, continues her stellar work as my in-house editor, tempering criticism with praise, always there whether a sounding board or a carpenter is required.

Finally, my longtime friend and agent Dominick Abel continues to be indispensable where his clients Mickey and Max are concerned. And thanks to James L. Traylor, co-author of our Edgar-nominated *Spillane: King of Pulp Fiction*, for keeping the Spillane flag flying.

MICKEY SPILLANE

In July of 2006, the last major mystery writer of the twentieth century left the building. Only a handful of writers in the genre – Agatha Christie, Dashiell Hammett, and Raymond Chandler among them – achieved such superstar status.

Spillane's position, however, is unique – reviled by many mainstream critics, despised and envied by a number of his contemporaries in the very field he'd revitalized, the creator of Mike Hammer had a profound impact not just on mystery and suspense fiction but popular culture in general.

The success of the reprint editions of his startlingly violent and sexually charged novels jump-started the paperback original, and his redefinition of the action hero as a tough guy who mercilessly executed villains and who slept with beautiful, willing women remains influential to this day (*Sin City* is Frank Miller's homage).

When Spillane published *I, the Jury* in 1947, he introduced in Mike Hammer the most famous of all fictional private eyes. Hammer swears vengeance over the corpse of an army buddy who lost an arm in the Pacific saving the detective's life. No matter who the villain turns out to be, Hammer will not just find him, but execute him – even if *he* turns out to be *her*.

This was something entirely new in mystery fiction, and Spillane quickly became the most popular – and controversial – mystery writer of the mid-twentieth century. He was called a fascist by left-leaning critics and a libertine by right-leaning ones. In between were millions of readers who turned Spillane's first six Hammer novels into the best-selling private eye novels of all time.

The controversial Hammer has been the subject of a radio show, comic strip, and several television series, starring Darren McGavin in the 1950s and Stacy Keach in the '80s and '90s. Numerous gritty movies have been made from Spillane novels, notably director Robert Aldrich's seminal film noir, *Kiss Me Deadly* (1955).

As success raged around him, Mickey Spillane proved himself a showman and a marketing genius; he became as famous as his creation, appearing on book jackets with gun in hand and fedora on head. His image became synonymous with Hammer's, more so even than any of the actors who portrayed the private eye, including McGavin and Keach.

For eighteen years, well past the peak of his publishing success, Spillane appeared as himself/Hammer in the wildly successful Miller Lite commercials, alongside his "Doll" (Lee Meredith of *The Producers* fame) and overshadowing countless former pro athletes.

Alone among mystery writers, he appeared as his own famous detective on screen, in the 1963 film *The Girl Hunters*. Critics at the time viewed his performance as Hammer favorably, and today many viewers of the quirky, made-in-England film still do. Virtually an amateur, Spillane is in nearly every frame, his natural charisma and wry humor holding him in good stead next to the professional likes of Lloyd Nolan (Michael Shayne of the '40s Fox movie series) and Shirley Eaton ("golden girl" of *Goldfinger*).

The Girl Hunters wasn't Spillane's first feature film – it wasn't even his first leading role in one. In 1954, John Wayne hired Spillane to star with Pat O'Brien and lion-tamer Clyde Beatty in *Ring of Fear*, a film he co-scripted without credit, receiving a white Jaguar as a gift from producer Wayne.

Revenge was a constant theme in Mike Hammer's world – *Vengeance is Mine!* among his titles – with the detective rarely taking a paying client. Getting even was the motivation for this detective. Mike Hammer paved the way for James Bond – *Casino Royale* in particular has its revenge aspect – and every tough action P.I., cop, lone avenger and government agent who followed, from Shaft to Billy Jack, from Dirty Harry to Jack Bauer. The latest Hammer-style heroes include an unlikely one – the vengeance-driven young woman of the Dragon Tattoo trilogy – as well as a more obvious descendent, Lee Child's Jack Reacher.

In the years since his first appearance in *I, the Jury* (1947), however, it seems ever more obvious: there is only one Mike Hammer.

And one Mickey Spillane.

MAX ALLAN COLLINS

Max Allan Collins collaborated with Mickey Spillane on numerous projects, including twelve anthologies, three films, and the *Mike Danger* comic book series.

Collins has also earned an unprecedented twenty-four Private Eye Writers of America "Shamus" nominations, winning for the novels *True Detective* (1983) and *Stolen Away* (1993) in his Nathan Heller series, and in 2013 for "So Long, Chief," a Mike Hammer short story begun by Spillane and completed by Collins. In 2024 he received the Strand Magazine Life Achievement award.

His classic graphic novel *Road to Perdition* (illustrated by Richard Piers Rayner) is the basis of the Academy Award-winning film directed by Sam Mendes and starring Tom Hanks, Paul Newman and Daniel Craig. Max's other comics credits include *Dick Tracy*; *Batman*; and with co-creator artist Terry Beatty, his own *Ms. Tree* and *Wild Dog*, the latter featured on the *Arrow* TV series.

Max's body of work includes film criticism, short fiction, songwriting, trading-card sets, and movie/TV tie-in novels, such as the *New York Times* bestseller *Saving Private Ryan*, numerous *USA Today*-bestselling *CSI* novels, and the Scribe Award-winning

American Gangster. His non-fiction includes *Scarface and the Untouchable: Al Capone* and *Eliot Ness & the Mad Butcher* (both with A. Brad Schwartz).

An award-winning filmmaker, he wrote and directed the Lifetime movie *Mommy* (1996) and five other features; his produced screenplays include the 1995 HBO World Premiere *The Expert* and *The Last Lullaby* (2008), based on his innovative Quarry novels, also the basis of *Quarry*, a Cinemax TV series.

Collins has written and directed two documentaries, *Caveman: V.T. Hamlin and Alley Oop* (2005) and his *Mike Hammer's Mickey Spillane* (1998) appears on the Criterion Collection release of the acclaimed film noir, *Kiss Me Deadly*, the latter receiving a 2024 updated expansion with a separate home-video release. A radio-style play, *Mickey Spillane's Encore for Murder*, starring Gary Sandy (*WKRP in Cincinnati*) as Hammer, was presented in Owensboro, Kentucky, and Clearwater, Florida, as well as the writer's hometown, Muscatine, Iowa, where a 2023 live performance was recorded and released as a video program.

Mickey Spillane appeared in two Collins films, *Mommy* (1995) and *Mommy's Day* (1997). Collins' most recent indie film is *Blue Christmas* (2024), in which Mickey Spillane's hat (given by Spillane as a gift to Collins) is worn by the lead actor, Rob Merrit. In 2024, the Collins novel *True Detective* was adapted by its author as a ten-part immersive audio drama directed by Robert Meyer Burnett and produced by Imagination Connoisseurs Unlimited.

As "Barbara Allan," he and his wife Barbara's collaborative novels include the "Trash 'n' Treasures" mystery series (recently *Antiques Foe*). Their novel *Antiques Flea Market* won the 2008

Toby Bromberg Award for Excellence for Most Humorous Mystery from *Romantic Times Book Review Magazine.* A film based on the series, *Death by Fruitcake*, scripted and directed by the Collinses, was produced in August 2024.

MIKE HAMMER NOVELS

In response to reader requests, I have assembled this chronology to indicate where the Hammer novels I've completed from Mickey Spillane's unfinished manuscripts and other materials fit into the canon. An asterisk indicates the collaborative works. J. Kingston Pierce of the fine website *The Rap Sheet* pointed out an inconsistency in this list (as it appeared with *Murder Never Knocks*) that I've corrected.

It should be noted that the prologue and epilogue of *Baby, It's Murder* make it the final Hammer chronologically; but the bulk of the book is a flashback to the early 1970s, as the introductory material asserts.

M.A.C.

Killing Town*
I, the Jury
Lady, Go Die!*
The Twisted Thing (published 1966, written 1949)
My Gun is Quick

MIKE HAMMER

Vengeance is Mine!
One Lonely Night
The Big Kill
Kiss Me, Deadly
Kill Me, Darling*
The Girl Hunters
The Snake
The Will to Kill*
The Big Bang*
Complex 90*
Murder Never Knocks*
The Body Lovers
Survival... Zero!
Kiss Her Goodbye*
The Killing Man
Masquerade for Murder*
Murder, My Love*
Black Alley
King of the Weeds*
The Goliath Bone*
Baby, It's Murder*

For more fantastic fiction, author events,
exclusive excerpts, competitions, limited editions and more

VISIT OUR WEBSITE
titanbooks.com

LIKE US ON FACEBOOK
facebook.com/titanbooks

FOLLOW US ON TWITTER AND INSTAGRAM
@TitanBooks

EMAIL US
readerfeedback@titanemail.com